Introduction

Some human beings can look wise; and some can actually even be wise. Some human beings can look like fools to the untrained observer as their great big plans go mysteriously off track. It's what makes us people. And we need to stop a moment, look back at life, and laugh where we can.

Sometimes we need to look back at life through the eyes of a child, so I looked back... with one eye closed and the other eye barely open.

To my surprise the grass was greener and taller, because the Canadian thistles were thriving! So I had to rub these spots out with the McVanBuck fix-it-all kit... fire. Mind you, a controlled wildfire. And the birds chirped louder, so loud that it got real annoying. I could not hear myself talk over their noisy chirping racket... so I had to write it down instead.

These stories are of the McVanBuck family. We are somewhat like them, for who hasn't tried to move a ladder without getting down from the top of the ladder first? It is called walking-the-ladder to save some time. I then miscalculated, fell nine feet, and broke an ankle... yes, there was that unforeseen excruciating pain and screaming that caught me a little by surprise, but this was fate as it gave me the time to write this book.

Thank you to everyone who truly understands and everyone who, at some point, has been stuck in a McVanBuck parallel universe for a day.

A big thanks also to Joy, my wife, and all of my kids who let me join their home-schooling class to do some art and writing for a season. These adventure stories are just good clean fun, and if I did a good job of writing them, then hopefully they will give you a few laughs.

Welcome to the McVanBuck family...

Contents

Chapter One

*

Sasquatch Chills

My eyes popped-open in a flash! I was awakened in the wee hours of the night, yet again. So I jumped out of bed, to be a hero who was being forced into action, like a blurry-eyed sleepwalker that was now spiked with a wave of adrenaline.

This midnight canter most commonly involved a number of things like: crying babies with unpleasant gas, a crying child that had a bad dream, and, of course, coming to the defence of our long-haired farm cat, named Smoky. Who, I might add, is a cat that looks much like a tangled-ball of Christmas lights. These tangles all over Smoky's body were done in an inside-out kind of way, so that no one can figure out for the life of them, which end his head is attached to. Just how Smoky's fur got into such a non-repairable state of tangly knots, is the ninth cat wonder of the world.

Untangling Smoky by jerking on two knots, one at each end of his body, is not a good option. As for a ball of tangled Christmas lights, it is worth giving it a few violent jerking shakes to attempt to untangle it, (even though this whipping action seldom untangles the ball of lights), but this rule cannot be applied to a cat.

The day came when we shaved Smoky bald to help him out. It was the only option left to us when he showed up back at our house after visiting his lady feline friend at Mr. Brown's farm down the road from us. He showed up looking like a tumble weed with legs, with thorny sticks embedded deep into his already knotted fur balls of hair. This shaving gave Smoky the clean look, but his naked body was getting the cold chills and he looked embarrassed walking around outside naked without some added secondary help.

I had tried to be compassionate at the time,

by cutting a hole in the toe of my sock for his head and four small holes for his legs. Then I attempted to stuff Smoky through the top end of the sock to make a little sweater for him. It's at this point that I would advise only attempting to put a sweater on a much friendlier city cat, it will save you a trip to the emergency room at the hospital.

But this kind of brilliant innovation, in showing a man's kind of love to the cat, only drew scowls from my wife, Joy, as she shook her head in disgust at my good idea.

She said, "You can't put the cat in your sock like that! What if the cat gets your nasty athlete's foot all over his whole body?"

I responded, "He would only get athlete's foot on one of his paws, for the fungus is only bad on my left foot. I could take my foot out of the sock to give him a little more room, would that help?"

At that I got an unwanted eye-roll of disdain from Joy, and a disgusted smacking noise came from her lips as she shook her head from side to side slightly.

It is hard to think outside of the box, beyond the common man's thinking... but it is also hard to not be the common man. It takes hard work and being tough enough to take an eye-roll or two from Joy, to bring in new ideas for all of mankind to enjoy.

Every week or so just like clock-work, at

some crazy hour of the night, Joy and I would get an unwanted visitor who thought that its sole duty in life was to torment us with weirdo noises that would give us no sleep. We could not, for the life of us, figure out what kind of critter insisted on tormenting us.

We knew that the odd sounding, creepy howl did a really good job of making all the hair on our arms and the back of our necks stand up. This awful sound which the critter of the night made was definitely on the spooky side of things, to say the least, for it was certainly no farm animal sound, like a mooing cow or a squealing pig. Sometimes, this would get Smoky, who was a tougher-than-nails tomcat, into quite a stir. This came with hissings, growling, and a very impressive, mean and fierce meowing. Smoky was, indeed, pulling his weight of work around our small farm in defending us against this creature that we had imagined to be Sasquatch and his posse of hairy outlaws.

These imaginings of a Big Foot were not outside the realm of relevant possibility, for the truth is I had seen Sasquatch once with my own two eyes, in northern British Columbia, Canada, near a small town called Pink Mountain. It could have been an large dead stump of a tree that was broken-off ten feet from the ground.

This Sasquatch-looking log had light brown fur and long hair on his head. His hair was a mess like he had just woke up from a bad night's sleep which had given him a bad case of bedhead, making his hair on the right side of his head stand straight up like a rooster's tail. He was just motionlessly standing there, about twenty yards away, staring at me and my hunting buddy Max.

That was all normal, until the log blinked! As our faces went pale, we ducked back down into the tall oat crop we had been standing in, and crawled as fast as we could back to the pick-up truck like a couple of frightened cowards. We thought it may have been a large, ugly grizzly bear with long hair on his head and paws with his monkey-like face to match, or it was just a log with a monkey face that was having a bad hair day.

Smoky was our guard dog on the lookout for strange, ugly ape-faced grizzly bears and was our front-line of defence against blinking logs. Smoky went toe-to-toe with smaller critters as well, like rats, raccoons, coyotes, and stray dogs, who would come in to our farmyard to kill our chickens and turkeys, or turn our garden inside out. This kept him busy while he waited to tangle with that Sasquatch, were he ever to show up in our yard. Sasquatch is real, but hardly anyone believes that Sasquatch exists. I will have to shoot one first, so I can prove that Sasquatch really lives. Once he is killed and dressed out, I can also prove, once and for all, that his meat isn't that bad tasting, if you use enough salt and barbecue sauce.

Joy should give me a good idea of what it tastes like when the time comes, but I will have to run that by her later, I am sure she wouldn't mind having the first taste test.

Joy has a special gift of hearing snaps and cracks coming from the outside, through the bedroom window, which many times, do not turn into much after she roots me out of our bed. A little hypothetical example of this would be, let's say, like an inexperienced first mate of a navy submarine who hears snaps and cracks through the earphones that are not important to the survival of the ship and crew. This crew member listens intently with her earphones on long enough, that she thinks she hears something out there that must be an enemy battleship or an aircraft carrier.

She says, "I...I... I think I hear something out there!"

This little sputter of words, throws the whole sub into red alert at 3 a.m.

The Captain of the sub, now woken from a peaceful sleep, goes into holding his breath for the next ten to fifteen minutes, listening intensely until his words break the silence after several tense moments with, "Joy, that's only a dumb dog barking again."

I mean, "All clear, only a school of fish," the Captain says sweetly and lovingly.

The captain now thinks of court-martialing this first mate and down right throwing her overboard to the school of barking fish.

Joy's nose isn't all that bad, either, while she is sleeping, when the neighbouring family of skunks make their weekly field trip under our open country-bedroom window.

Joy has a routine of waking me up, after hearing such strange noises and smells outside, with some solid jabs to my ribs.

She would say, after waking me up, "Do you smell that? I think it's a skunk... that stinks. E*www! Yuck*!"

I would reply by saying, "Yes, I can smell it, now that I am wide awake... but I was quite immune to it when I was still nicely sleeping."

The captain had to outright outlaw solid night-time jabs to the ribs after the unfortunate accident, that I can still remember like it was yesterday. I remember this part very clearly. I had spent the early part of the night restless, tossing and turning in my sleep. This had gotten me all turned around in our king-size bed, before I was able to go soundly to sleep.

Once asleep I began to dream, and in my

dream I was a happy kid, minding my own business, joyfully playing in the school yard with the other kids. Then a little pretty girl, named Penny, came springing out from the branches of the tree above and landed right in front of me. She was so sweet and I was enamoured with her, and I wanted her to be my girlfriend... *"ahh"*.

Then, without warning, her face turned nasty and a menacing mean grin abruptly appeared on her face, that was overlapping her big mouth full of braces. Her face then changed into a painful turnip that made my eyes water and turned my smile sideways.

Without warning, she had given me the hardest kick to my crotch. It was such a hard, painful kick for a dream. It felt so real, it could have easily registered very high on the Richter scale for an earthquake.

This painful nightmare flooded my mind, and this unpleasant dream seemed to go into slow-mo. Then the unexpected, second thundering blow of death came upon me before I could catch my breath from the first blow. This time, though, I could definitely tell that this was not a dream at all! As I forced my eyes awake, it was like the lights on a car coming alive in the darkness. I was trying to make my brain tell my lips to speak words of surrender, while at the same time, tell my arms to get untangled from the blanket that had me pinned to the bed.

I was caught like a fly in a spider's web. It was essential to get my arms free and into a defensive position to protect the precious family jewels, but by the third blow of death below my belt, I could hear Joy whispering in the darkness, "Are you awake yet?"

I was now sputtering out words that signified I was indeed wide-awake, but felt like death had arrived. I freed myself from the blankets by using all of my remaining strength to push my arms and legs out through the sheets, like the mighty moth freeing itself from its cocoon of a prison.

Then I caught my breath and was able to regain the gift of speech after several breathless, excruciating minutes. I recalled to Joy the horrifying nightmare that had just unfolded out of my peaceful sleep and how the blankets had me pinned in a torture-stretch.

Naturally, she was shocked and embarrassed, “Oh no, I am terribly sorry!” She said, “I was not aware that you were lying in such a vulnerable position.”

She insisted that she really thought her elbow was jabbing a couple of ribs, as she sheepishly handed me the bag of ice that she had retrieved from the freezer. I just laid there for several minutes, moaning and groaning, while grabbing my knees in the fetal position. This was to give the needed time for life to re-enter my body.

Joy then went on to explain the reason why she was trying to wake me up in the first place. It seemed that the spine-chilling Sasquatch was now in our yard. She could hear it clearly and needed me to go out there and “shoot it”.

I did not really want to go after this elusive beast again. For every time this spine-tingling monster tested it’s weekly mating call of sorts on the cat, I would get up, pry the sleep from my eyes, get dressed, and run out the front door, armed and ready for some sort of wild action -- to tangle against ape-face himself. But by the time I would get outside, I would hear absolutely nothing, except for maybe the occasional frogs croaking and the mosquitoes buzzing in my ears.

After walking around the barnyard a bit and waiting for an hour or more out there, I would shrug my shoulders, go back into the house, and put the gun back in its cabinet. I would then get undressed and crawl back into bed and try for the next two hours to make myself go back to sleep, while trying to shake the thoughts of Sasquatch trying to catch Smoky out of my head.

So this time I said, "Just go back to sleep, sweetheart, and forget about the bone-chilling screech..." The howls from this critter sounded like a screech-scream and a whoop, mixed with a low, sinister, cackling undertone.

It did not help to tell Joy to just ignore the echoing racket that was now escalating outside to new proportions, for the sounds were starting to get my attention, also.

Joy said, "I think the monster's really got a hold of Smoky, this time!"

She did have a point, the cat did sound like he was in over-his-head and in big trouble, in fending off the unknown tormentor. I figured I should, at least, give another swing at a cat rescue, as compassion kicked in. I would come to the aid of our cat for my wife's sake. Even though I knew that the cat, in five minutes, would be all miraculously curled up in a peaceful ball, soundly sleeping on the porch by the time I got out the front door, just like all the other times that I made an effort at being a hero.

So after the pain left my body, I got the gun from the gun cabinet with a yawn. I headed out the bedroom door. There was no point in putting on my shoes or clothes, for that matter, because I would be back in a moment anyways, after I poked my head outside the porch door. The boxer shorts that I had on would be more than sufficient for this routine summertime canter on a warm night.

I left the bedroom with Joy's voice trailing behind me, "You be careful out there now, it really sounds scary!"

"You got it. I'll get ape-face this time, I got my big gun," came my reply.

So I pushed open the screen door leading to the outside world with my foot, and stumbled out the front door. I rubbed the sleep out of my eyes with another yawn, the gun lazily tucked under my arm like a sleeping baby. I could hear the critter also, and it did sound like it was even closer to the yard then all the other times. This was about the thirtieth time I had done this midnight walk and found nothing outside.

According to the routine plan in my mind, I took a few steps down the sidewalk in my bare feet. I could feel the coldness of the concrete under my feet. I stopped a moment to look at the billion stars shining down on me from the moonless, clear sky as a falling star shot by. This brought a smile to my face, but I was not going to spend much of my sleeping time out there this night looking at the stars. I was about to head back inside, before all the sleep completely evaporated from my eyeballs, when strangely, I thought I actually heard something! It was rattling in the darkness off to my right, louder than my now-chattering teeth. This rattling was coming from the nearby woods.

I now came to full attention in that direction. An uneasy lump in my throat was suddenly making an unexpected appearance. The gun came from the lazy cradle-hold to a ready position, with my finger twitching on the trigger, as my other hand pulled the hammer back to bring the gun to a ready-and-loaded state for the mayhem and wild action to come. In a moment, I saw something coming up the driveway beside the pickup truck, out of the darkness and into the yard light, with great haste.

As the critter came into the light, my heart-rate was now on a speedy rise, along with the hair on the back of my neck, which was trying to outrace my racing heart that was pounding in my chest.

I sighed a big sigh, "Whew," when I saw that it was only Smoky. I said to Smoky, "You funny cat, you scared the happiness out of me," and I shook my head in relief.

Instinctively, I licked the palm of my hand, and followed this by combing down the hair on the back of my neck that was now standing straight up like the hair on the back of a wild, razorback hog. I assumed that Smoky had heard me step out of the house and was now coming in for a midnight snack, a petting, or something like that. Strangely, he did not even seem to see or hear me, as he ran straight between my bare legs. I found this very perplexing, and I followed him with my eyes as he ran behind me through the lilac hedge beside the house at a speed that was just a click shy of greased lightning.

I have never seen greased lightning firsthand before, to compare it accurately, but I believe it would stand as greased lightning for Smoky slipped through my legs like grease out of a grease gun.

Very odd behaviour, maybe he's in heat? I thought to myself. Yet, I knew from Smoky's undercarriage, that he was indeed a "he" and not a "she"; I had learned this from being raised as a farm kid. I also knew that only those of the female variety could be "in heat." At least now, one could soundly conclude that Smoky was indeed a very odd cat. It was odd, indeed, for him to be making all those bone chilling noises, all by himself.

I guess our weekly midnight monster is this tomcat of ours, I now reckoned to myself. This cat, of course, would've had to swallow a handful of rusty nails to sound as spooky as the monster, but I guess anything is possible.

I gave a nervous, halfhearted laugh and a jittery gulp, as I tried to make myself believe this strange conclusion. Uneasy and not completely satisfied, I turned to head back inside the house.

Then without warning, the beast was now coming straight at me, out from the dark woods where Smoky had just come from. It was running fast and smooth. I aimed my rifle roughly at a six-foot height, but then I re-thought the height. If this was indeed a Sasquatch, I would want that critical first shot to be a headshot to bring him to the ground in a single shot, for what would he do to me if I only wounded him? So I aimed higher. It is better to be safe than sorry, especially when weird noises are coming from the woods towards you. Suddenly, the tormenting beast reared up his ugly head and raced into the yard light. The frightening figure rushed at me very quickly, even faster than Smoky's greased lightning!

To my shock, a hideous old red fox, that looked like it had a real bad case of mange, was coming right at me! Mange is a disease which foxes, coyotes, and other critters get which causes the hairy critter to lose their hair in patches, kind of like the premature balding on some men.

The fox must have been spooked out of the woods by the Sasquatch as well, so I aimed my gun even higher! This fox's tongue was hanging out of the one side of his mouth, half-way to the ground. He had what looked like a pretty-jolly smile on his face from the joy of torturing the cat. It was becoming apparent to me that this was the real tormentor, so I readjusted my gun for a much smaller target, about ten feet lower from where I had been aiming my gun.

Pretty quickly, I realized that this fox, like Smoky, did not see me standing there on the sidewalk. This time, I was not about to let this crazed fox pass through my bare legs like Smoky had, or a Sasquatch either, if he was still out there in the darkness. So, I dug deep in my throat and belched out a high-pitched squalling shriek, hitting notes along the way that I thought only sopranos could reach.

In the process of doing this, I bolted upwards into a gigantic, sky-high jumping-jack, just in case the fox did not hear the high-pitch voice that was performing a perfect duet with the rifle that was somehow singing out shells into the night in no-particularly fancy direction. I suppose my finger was still dancing on the hair trigger of the gun.

The poor mangy fox, on the other hand, must have found this equally frightening to his heart, to find his enemy standing with a gun a mere two feet away.

The fox must have been thinking to himself, *How can I be seeing the cat instantly turn into a lunatic human-being, singing opera and blasting shells into the cool night air, while doing wild, gymnastic splits in his underwear?*

The fox's body was instantly thrown into a very impressive, breaking handstand in an all-out-attempt to bring himself to a stop as his mouth and tongue hit the sidewalk underneath himself. At the same time, he was trying to use his legs like some sort of hysterical pinwheels in reverse, which threw dust my way.

Bringing myself back from the dead, I reestablished my heart into a working order, as it was now running laps inside my chest. The fox streaked into the night, away from me. My composure now recaptured, I pulled my legs back under myself. I got up off the sidewalk from this unnatural sitting position, known as the splits, where I had made my unexpected landing.

If I had only known that I was going to be confronted so closely by a mere small fox and not a two thousand-pound Sasquatch, I would have grabbed the smaller .22 calibre gun instead of my much larger .30-06 rifle.

The .30-06 is a fine gun, if you wanted to bring down a raving mad, snot-flinging, charging Sasquatch, but not necessarily for a half-crazed, jolly old fox with his tongue hanging out of his mouth.

I made my way back into the house, shaking off the dust of fright. Joy was there to meet me, her eyes the size of frying-pans staring out from a ghostly complexion.

She followed me to the bedroom, stuttering out her feelings that she thought I had encountered the Sasquatch and that he had torn off my arms and proceeded to eat the rest of me alive before my gun started going off, because she heard a very different scary Sasquatch shriek just before the gun started firing off.

Joy then changed the topic in mid-thought and asked, "What are you doing there in your underwear drawer?"

I replied, "Just getting a change of boxer-shorts."

"Wow, did Sasquatch do that to you?" she

asked, as she continued without giving me a moment to fully explain.

"They're split right through to the waistband, and just look at your backside!

Why are you walking so stiff-legged?

Did he give you those nasty scrapes all the way down the inside of your legs? Boy, are you going to feel that in the morning! Did you get the Sasquatch? You did get him... right?"

I answered, "Well, I may have wounded him..." One of the bullets could have hypothetically hit him when it fell down out of the sky... sooner or later.

Now the fox or the Sasquatch, of course, would have to be right under the bullet, as it came back down to earth. This could have easily wounded the fox, if the stars lined up just right. Of course, this wouldn't be very likely, but never-the-less, it is technically possible in the eyes of an optimistic McVanBuck.

The next morning, I painfully hobbled past our truck in the driveway, on my way to do the barn chores. There were many *ecks* and *ouch's* along the way. For apparently, it was my legs that were not trained to do the splits anymore, like they had been in high-school. My legs just wanted to stay in that position... straight out.

I could clearly see where the poor love-bug fox had left a good chunk of fox scat on the lawn, beside the two skid-marks. I guess I scared the fox a bit too much. There are times in life where certain faces stick in your head forever, and this fox's frowning face of love-horror is etched into my mind as much as my jumping-jacks would be stuck in his mind.

After chores, I got the shovel and with a few more *ecks* and *ouch's* in my wobble, I cleaned up the mess off of our lawn that our night-time fox had uncontrollably dropped.

I needed the shovel because the scat from him was as large as a cow pie, so I couldn't just run it over with the lawnmower, and it wasn't small enough to just rub into the earth with the heel of my shoe. Perhaps my eyes were playing tricks on me and it wasn't a mangy fox at all, but a mangy baby Sasquatch with a full stomach and weak bowels when faced with fear.

One will never know if it was truly a fox, for he came in so fast and was so ugly. And who would truly believe me that a fox can, indeed, mimic the eerie echo howl of the Sasquatch?

Back in the house, I found Joy at the table pouring some strong coffee straight into her sleepless eyelids.

After a couple of sips, Joy then commented, "Well, the good news is you got some good shots off at Sasquatch to keep him away from me. I didn't get a wink of sleep last night with all the screaming, shooting, and the weirdo noises that Sasquatch was making."

I replied, "I was more thinking that this is why we just close our eyes real tight and go back to sleep, and let Sasquatch just do his thing."

Chapter Two

**

Fire Fools

It is truly unexplainable why fire takes an unexpected wrong turn down Destruction Avenue and up Charcoal Street.

Fire has a mind of her own, and I have been experimenting, trying to figure out her mind for many years. I am merely following in the footsteps of my McVanBuck kin, who have experimented with fire before me. It took Thomas Edison a hundred and one failures before he could get the light bulb to light up, and educated people still call him a genius, but they insult us by calling us McVanBucks fools.

One saving hope of rehabilitation for ones like myself is that in recent years, I have moved out into the countryside. This way, the semi-controlled grass fires have to be gigantic and nasty before people get all stirred up and running with a water hose in hand.

In the city, if you make one wee little mistake and underestimate the wind conditions, it can take no time all to see an inexplicably angry neighbour, acting like he has never seen a fire before.

City folk then make you look “real bad,” as you find out that you’re on the front page of the city newspaper the next morning, dressed in your bathrobe, looking like a coal miner with wide-eyes of panic. Fire trucks are there in the background, of course, but more for show and a chance to gawk at a burnt patch of grass than anything else.

This was all setting the scene to make the wee little fire look bigger than it really was. This overzealous act of city folks to put out the semi-controlled fire, which was no bigger than a raging campfire in my eyes, can be confusing to some.

For some unknown reason, city folks just don’t like it one bit, to wake-up in the morning smelling smoke and a fire alarm going off in their ears! They, being now promptly awakened from their peaceful city sleep, begin smelling the burning wood and plastic smoke that is billowing into their open window.

They leap out of bed to find outside their window, a mad man (in their minds) in his bathrobe whacking at his small semi-controlled grass fire that is now burning their rotten fence along with their storage shed down to the ground at 6 a.m. (even though this fence was clearly rotten and needed burning down at some point anyways).

Well, that goes at least for their fence... their brand new $1200 shed could have been spared... I suppose. I tried my best to help my neighbour look at the bright side of it all, and I put my arm across his shoulders to comfort him as we looked at his burned up and blackened backyard.

I said to him, "At least you can start fresh with a new fence... and you don't need to waste your time this weekend painting that new shed..."

I also tried to cheer him up, by opening his can of paint for him free of charge, but the paint was just a dried lump that looked like a red kiln-fired brick in the bottom of the can. This just made my neighbour weep big tears as he stared into the can.

It was at this point, I figured, I would just slowly back away from the burnt rubble and let the fire insurance adjusters sort out what was still salvageable or not. Perhaps, his wife would let him cry on her shoulder. He was starting to make me feel guilty, like I had done something wrong. I was pretty sure his fire insurance covered "Acts of God".

Now, if only those city folks could have seen some of the massive McVanBuck fires - now those were real intense fires from my youth on my family's farm - they probably would have over-reacted as well, but for a really good reason this time. As a youth, our neighbours had no shortage of excitement to see, from both far and wide, in the direction of our family farm.

It was a well-established fact, built up over the years while growing up in our area, that whenever so much as a curl of smoke came from our McVanBuck family farm, the neighbours instinctively knew to just start running for the telephone to call in the water-bomber planes, choppers, and the national guard to fight the fire. I suppose, if there had been speed-dial at that time, the fire department would have been on it. My two younger brothers and I caught the firebug fever honestly from our firebug dad.

Our dad, Elvis, was a hard-working farmer. He had a strong, muscular, shorter body; a very large nose; and very large and distinctive, black furry lamb-chop side-burns to match his half-balding, curly head of hair.

Dad had a very special relationship with fire, kinda like a bad marriage. She, the "fire," would always get overheated and get things way out-of-control at the least sight of engagement. Then she, with a fiery head of steam, would run like the wind into no particular, adjacent neighbour's yard to destroy everything in her path.

The fiery marriage would always end in the same manner, with some four hundred neighbours coming in from three counties. The neighbours would arrive in cars and pickup trucks, which were carrying barrels of water on the back of their trucks. There would also arrive at our yard a good number of tractors pulling plows and discs.

The neighbours would come with the typical fire-fighting equipment like shovels, pick-axes, and water buckets. Most times, the shovels and pick-axes were still on the back of their pickups from the last fire visit to our yard.

As for the tractors, they were plucked straight out of the fields, where they were calmly working their slow, mundane routine just minutes earlier, and were now thrust into some real action. The neighbours, of course, came to help fight the blazing inferno of a fire, or to gawk and chatter with the onlookers at this yearly reunion of sorts.

They would chat with each other, saying, “Hokey smokes! Now, this is a bonfire! It’s even bigger than last year’s fire, and look at that, they were even able to burn down that whole clump of woods...”

“Yep, that’s something alright...” the tall neighbour would reply, while leaning on a half burned-off shovel.

He continued, “Oh boy, look at that! Let’s wander over there and see that barley field back there, where all the running action is at now... I think, I see smoke over there... Yep, that is fire alright... must have jumped their fire barrier.”

The short farmer would respond with wide-eyes of surprise, “Cripes, let’s get moving then... that’s my barley field!”

And the toothpick that he had been lazily chewing on, was quickly spat out of his mouth, as he started in that direction at a full run towards his now burning crops.

Yet, others said things like, “Shoot! Wow... did you say that their propane tanks are on fire?” as we, the red-faced McVanBuck family, would be panicking and frantically racing this way and that, with picks, shovels, and buckets of water.

The intense glowing of our faces was naturally from the fierce heat of the fires and the marathon of steps ran, hauling pails full of water, and not due to just embarrassment like some would have you believe.

My genetic firebug mutation all started with my dad, Elvis McVanBuck, when he was just a kid. He started his trade by burning Grandpa McVanBuck's "stuff" down to the ground by accident.

One day, Dad was in a story-time mood. He told us of his first fiery event that went more or less sideways when he was a wee lad, by saying, "Ya see, there was these bees and these bees needed a kill'in, so me and my little brother burned d'em out... what else could we do? ...they'd stung me already and almost got my little brother!"

I thought for a second and was about to speak of other alternatives, like using a can of spray to kill the bees, when Dad cut my first word short. He probably thought I was about to sneeze with my big inhale.

"That's right... nothing could've been done, but a burn'in d'em bees out of their nest that was in some straw bales. Sure, a few straw bales got burnt up... yes, but d'em bees didn't sting another innocent little kid like me and my little brother."

Later that week, I asked Grandpa McVanBuck what had happened when the bees got burned up. I defended my dad at

first and said, "The evil bees had stung him and almost got his little brother, so he burned out the bees to death."

Grandpa McVanBuck replied, "Burn d'em? The bees Elvis was trying to burn out, were in straw bales, alright, located in the hay loft of my barn! Cripes, the barn burned down to the ground in one horrific fireball of flames. Those two boys of mine barely 'scaped out of the burning barn alive. We barely had time to save the milk cows. Cripes, there was this stupid pig, who wasn't even in the barn at the time when the fire started, and he decided to run into the burning barn... of all the madness in this world, this pig leads them all... he didn't make it... he became early bacon."

I asked, "Grandpa? Do pigs go to heaven and become angel pigs?"

He answered, "No, no, just bacon and ham."

It was at this point, I realized, that my mind was playing tricks on me, for I had envisioned in my head that these bees, which my dad had burned, were in some bales, like in an open field. I started thinking, maybe I really had caught the viral disease going around that our mom called "selective hearing" after all... but at least I knew that the angels would be eating some good bacon and honey-smoked ham.

Chapter Three

⁂

Fuel Tank Fire

One spring, when I was in my youth, a fire started out just like the rest of all the other infernos... with the smell of fire fever in the air! Flames would soon be at hand, for both Nedge and I would be most certainly disappointed if we didn't get, at the very least, one meagre fire in the bag for the year.

With a good promising sign of smoke out in the backyard, Nedge and I made our way over to the source of the smoke. Elvis, my good old dad, was hard at work burning a small patch of grass behind the house. He had learned from his past experience that he should not leave a fire for one second with us firebug kids around, until it was out, dead-cold.

So Dad stood by as the fire burned itself out and nothing remained, except for a couple of small, smouldering hot-spots. We boys were looking on, just itching for some excitement for the day. After a while, Dad started to glance at his watch, like he had something else planned for the day.

Finally, after what seemed like eternity to us, he went into the house without saying a word, but he did give us a long, glaring look. We could only assume, this meant it was up to us to have a go at the fire on our own.

With that we sprang into action, to make an attempt at getting that stone-cold fire going again, this time with the added challenge of it being technically “out”.

We boys had an amazing gift, though, of being able to resurrect a stone-cold fire from the dead and into a small inferno. Within a few minutes and without matches, we had that cold fire going again by giving it some tender love and mouth-to-mouth resuscitation by blowing on it from our whistle-hole, until we felt like we were going to faint.

Just add some dead grass and *presto*, a

bonfire was kindled. Like a great evangelist that could raise the dead, we too could raise a fire from the dead. A couple of high-fives all around, and then off we went into the woods to get some more dead wood that just needed burning, we figured.

My brother Nedge, who was much huskier than my tall slender build, was a good thirty pounds heavier than myself, even though he was a year younger. He had a head like a millstone in shape, but with corners and it was as hard as a millstone as well.

My head is still swirling from the last knock my head had against his skull some thirty years ago.

Nedge got a bit excessive and carried away, at times, with adding all sorts of dry fuel to the fire, particularly when he would go too far by throwing my perfectly good toys into the fire, for he had a way of doing things before he thought of the consequences.

Don't get me wrong here, toys burned up real fine with a bit of added excitement when they were his toys, like a handful of his GI. Joes getting nuked in a re-enactment of World War II; but not when the toys were my toys.

I emerged from the woods carrying a stick, just shy of what some people may call a log. A log classification would be a big stick that needed two kids to carry it to the fire in my classifications of sticks.

I could see that Nedge's mind was already zealously fast at work on a greater scheme. He could see that there were other things around the yard that needed burning down to the ground before the day was done, besides my toys... I still miss that toy truck from time to time. Other worthless things lying around the yard that were not currently being used, like Mom's lawn chair, some plastic flower pots, and a variety of other useless garden supplies were his prime targets for fuelling the hunger of this fire.

Nedge, being the fire chief in charge on this labour of love of ours, had the worthless plastic junk already loaded onto the fire, which was burning quite intensely for a simple grass fire. It was growing into the size of a small car. He then began spreading this fiery excitement to feed the fire's lust and its need to get even bigger. His new visionary plan was beginning to take shape.

In preparation to take the fire in a new direction, like all great minds, he was laying out little clumps of dry grass, in a row, spaced about three feet apart. The grass clumps, being no bigger than a bag of popcorn in size, would be like stepping stones and markers on a treasure map leading to where the "X" would mark the spot of the great, unbelievable treasure.

This was done in a brilliant fashion to cross a pesky gravelled barrier that we called our driveway, for Nedge's great mind could understand that gravel and dirt do not burn. This unwanted hindrance needed a mastermind, like himself, to get the fire to cross from our side of the driveway to the other side, where it was needed. This had me intrigued, as I could start to see the framework of a high-tech math equation being worked into some sort of physics.

Without saying anything, because I did not want to bother someone so hard at work, I followed closely behind Nedge, trying to piece together his great, exciting new plan. I would hate to distract the mastermind at work and cause him to make a calculated mistake and burn up more of my toys.

I watched with fascination as Nedge gathered together a large handful of dry grass which he held over the fire that we had just resurrected and set the handful of grass ablaze. Holding the flaming handful of grass in his hand like a torch, he ran over to the row of grass clumps laying across the driveway. Nedge squatted down and used his fiery torch to quickly light the first pile of dry grass on fire.

Then he dropped the handful of grass that was now singeing his fingertips and waved his singed fingers in the air while doing a nice little tap-dance and howling, "Yeeooww!" Then he huffed and puffed on his fingers to cool his fingertips down, with urgent wind blowing from his lips, while shaking his hand.

Nedge's plan was really coming together and I could see the reason for the separated dry piles of grass. He moved from clump to clump, setting one clump on fire before moving onto the next.

Since the flaming grass in his hand burned very quickly, the piles gave him just enough time to light a new torch and carry it to the next pile of dead grass in the row crossing the driveway, before the flames started seriously gnawing at his fingertips. If the fire started chewing on his fingertips too quickly he would be forced to toss the fiery torch out of his hand.

This is where Nedge's full plan was starting to make sense to me. Dad had neglected to burn the real problem grass under the suspended fuel tanks that were on the other side of the driveway where there was tons of tall dead grass. This spot of ground was home to the dreaded, wicked Canadian thistles, burning nettle, and an assortment of other dry, cruel weeds. These fuel tanks were seated on stands made from wooden beams, to hold the tanks ten feet off the ground. The tanks were suspended up off of the ground to make it easier for the large farm equipment to get re-fuelled. This spot of weedy ground underneath these tanks was a nasty spot to play in and badly needed burning to rid our lives of this painful eyesore.

The last fire torch was chomping at Nedge's fingers as he ran to race the biting flames to cross the final span of road... or maybe it was just that Nedge was in a hurry to burn up all the weeds before Dad came back outside again to steal all the fun for himself.

Nedge tossed the final clump of grass that was in his hand into the unsightly patch of weeds and grass. As he did this, a strange thing happened; the grass burst into flames, but with such intensity that we had to step back a few feet to keep the flames from eating our faces off. The heat was so intense that it felt like a blowtorch was set against us.

"Wow, Nedge!" I exclaimed. "Now that's one big fire!" as the weeds were licked up by the flames in a flash like a bomb had just gone off.

After a few moments, the fire did not calm down like one would expect with normal grass fires, but instead, got far more intense as the flames were now licking at the poles of the two fuel tanks with a great deal of heat and cruel violence. I figured that the thirty empty plastic oil containers sitting under the fuel tanks that had been discarded over the years, were adding to the fireball.

This inferno raged yet hotter still, as the many gallons of gas that had been spilled on the ground from the fuel tanks over the years, added to the burning flames. One could clearly reckon, at this point, that thistles and weeds love the taste of gasoline and diesel to grow on, but fire had a sick lust infatuation to the gas that made our stomachs turn inside of us.

The lust of this fire was still not satisfied as I realized the fire was now drinking up the seven full five-gallon buckets of used oil sitting under the fuel tanks, to up its intensity!

This used oil had been collected over the course of years, from tractors, trucks, and anything that used oil, and was put into these five-gallon buckets and then put under the fuel tanks for lack of knowing what to do with them.

These were the days before recycling used oil made any sense at all, so the farmers would just put the old used oil in five-gallon buckets and then store them under their fuel tanks. This storage spot was chosen because, well...where else would you put the buckets? You couldn't just dump the old oil down an old well or in a creek, that would be just silly.

In the end, though, this fire event was a good learning lesson for my dad Elvis and he re-thought his plan for used oil. He changed the storage spot, and never stored the used-oil buckets under the fuel tanks again... he instead safely stored them in a small building. This building was not being used anymore, so he wisely put the full buckets of used-oil on some rotting boards that he placed over a large hole in the ground that was only the old water-well which was no longer in use.

The now looming massive fire-ball above Nedge and I roared on upwards, surrounding the two steel fuel tanks in front of us. This once-starved fire was now barking out the most frightening, billowing-black smoke that you could ever imagine. In moments, the once clear sky was filled with daunting, frightening clouds of smoke that sent chills up and down our youngsters' backs.

The fire under the gasoline tank was burning stronger and more intensely than the fire under the diesel tank, but the fire under the diesel tank was not all that far behind in the race to utter destruction and mayhem. At this moment, Nedge and I looked at each other, face to face, and each of us saw a mirror of horror and fear staring straight back at us. There are times in life when you realize that you got yourself into a wee bit of a predicament that was literally way up over your head. This, indeed, was one of those moments.

We then started to bolt in the direction of the house in a single accord of utter panic, where we could see Dad was already making his own bolting, giant strides of fear in our direction. He still had shaving cream on half of his face, as he ran like a world-class sprinter in his newly-purchased, tall rubber boots. You would not have guessed it, but he could run like the wind, even on a bad pair of knees that squeaked like rusty wheels on an old runaway train. I closed my eyes tightly, as he drew close to me, and I prepared for the promised land. Surprisingly, Dad just blew past both Nedge and me. Maybe there was something a little higher on his priority-list than dealing with us two boys at that moment.

Some kids have brave dads alright, but not as brave as mine. Dad leapt straight into the blazing inferno of the fire, and went for the taps on the tanks in an attempt to turn off the fuel tanks' shutoff valves. If the valves were not shut off soon, they would start to fuel the fire to even greater, unthinkable heights. Dad got the diesel tank valve shut off first, and then he went for the red-hot gasoline tank valve.

The gas valve was not so easy to turn off,

because now the fire was getting more intense in front of the tank, and well... the tap was getting hot, really hot! Fire likes to chew up gasoline much more intensely than diesel.

So Dad went at turning off this tap, one little turn at a time before he had to let go and shake his smoking, sizzling hand for a moment. Then he would crank at it some more. It was like he was grabbing a red-hot baked potato, while singing a chorus that we could hear quite clearly over the unthinkable roaring noise of the fire.

Dad's hand made a sizzling sound, like steak freshly placed on a hot barbecue, and he sang out, yelling, "*YEEOOOWOWEOW*... BOY, ARE YOU EVER HOT!!! HOT!!! HOT!!!... *YEEOOOWOWEOW*..."

As he finished closing the valve, the fuel hose that was connected to the tank burned right off at the valve and fell nicely down into his new, now-melting rubber boots, just like a Christmas gift tucked neatly into the mouth of a Christmas stocking. This caused him to leap out of the fire with an added jump in his stride. He resembled a wild and untamed, flailing animal, jumping like a one-legged bullfrog.

He was now bouncing for all he was worth, like a man with a focused mission on a pogo stick, to extinguish the flames in the one boot

that was now on fire and trying to burn his foot off, from the inside out. This hopping was added to his already violently flailing arms which were flapping like the wings of a large ostrich that could not get a total take-off, higher than three feet into the air. The flailing of Dad's arms was his attempt to cool his smoking hands that were now looking more like well-toasted buns and had grill-marks like two tasty steaks on an open grill.

As he was doing his less-than-festive, new-found song and dance, the diesel tank made a low ominous, but distinctive and noticeable, thundering *boom* much like a growl from the depths of a hungry stomach. Immediately, the tank had grown spheres on each end, instead of the normal flat ends of this 1,000-gallon fuel tank. It was now looking more like a submarine than a fuel tank.

At this moment, Mom broke onto the scene, running from the house with great speed as well. She was carrying two large five-gallon buckets of water that were defying the laws of gravity as they trailed straight out behind her. As she reached Dad, Dad's fiery leg went right into one of the buckets. I am sure, he would have jumped in headfirst into this bucket if there had been enough room for all of him to fit inside, for even his jacket hem was smoking from the savage, gnawing flames. As the bucket smoked with steam,

Dad's hands -- looking like fried steaks -- joined his leg in the pail of water.

Dad now barked a new order to Mom, "Becky... GET THE GUN!"

Even though he had more than a dozen rifles and guns, there was only one "gun" – the .300 calibre Winchester rifle that hung on the wall. I protested with great sorrow and pleaded with Mom to not let him do "it," as she ran back to the house in great haste.

Things are still fixable, I thought, *and maybe the massive fire ball, now lording over our farm, isn't as bad as it looks.*

I figured that Dad could not take the pain of his burned hands and foot anymore and was going to put himself out of his misery, like how a compassionate farmer needs to put the faithful, yet irreparably lame bull out of his agony.

Or the other equally bad ending was that he was going to put Nedge and I out of our misery. This would put an end to our antics and his despair, once and for all.

Of course, I was drawing the wrong conclusions. Dad may have thought it, but that was not the intent of the big gun that was now so badly needed.

Mom came back out of the house at a fervent pace, with a worried look on her face. The .300 calibre Winchester rifle was cradled in her arms, and she was currently loading it with ammunition as she ran towards Dad. Dad was painfully hopping his way to the house. It was then, I noticed, the loving neighbours were pouring into our yard and were filling it to overflowing as cars and trucks parked everywhere, even on the lawn, for the climax of the main event.

The distress signal, up above in the sky, was so large that no one needed directions to our farmyard. The excessively large black plume of smoke, that lorded over the farm like a massive thundercloud, led the way.

Dad, with his blistered red hands, took the gun from Mom and aimed it at the diesel tank that was looking more like a submarine. We watched with utmost dread as the tank appeared to be at the point of bursting, with self-destruction to be its end.

At this junction, I could now hear our elderly neighbour Mrs. Cooper, who lived just down the road from us, praying with great might; she rested her hands on my shoulders as she stood behind me. Her prayer went something like, “Dear God, help us now, before Elvis kills us all!”

As the bullets blazed off through the air at the fuel tanks, I could now see the wisdom behind Mrs. Cooper’s praying. And I also joined into the praying, for she was, indeed, right on target... Dad was trying to do us in -- all at the same time!

I closed my eyes for a second time, waiting for the coming promised land. What I didn't know, was that Dad, in reality, was saving all of our lives from the impending doom, peril, and death which brewed inside the diesel tank that was due to explode at any moment.

Dad's rifle shots released the growing pressure of gases from the diesel tank just in time, and the gases hissed out of the bullet holes in the tank. Moments later, the diesel stand burned right through, casting the now violently hissing tank to the ground with an ominous *THUD-BOOM!* I closed my eyes tight a third time, for what felt like a lifetime of horrors. This time, I was sure the promised land was at hand as the tears flowed down my cheeks. The ominous *THUD-BOOM* was a sound that drove to the core of even the toughest man, as we all instinctively sheltered our heads with our hands and arms. Thankfully, at this junction, like a miracle from above, the tank slowly rolled away from the intense fire and onto the driveway, where Nedge and I had first crossed the road with his burning-grass torch.

Mere moments later, Dad had a new target in the scope of his gun; this target was the remaining gasoline fuel tank which was still resting ten feet off the ground on the burning wooden stands. Another shot rang out from

Dad's big gun, as he aimed at the top part of the gasoline tank where the gas fumes were building up to great proportions inside. Dad's shot blasted a hole in the gasoline tank much like the hole he had shot in the diesel tank, moments earlier.

This new hole, that the bullet created in this tank, caused the tank to whistle violently with a chilling hiss. This squealing sound coming out of the tank, made the tank to scream with hideous agony like it was about to die. We knew it as well, that the tank was about to burst its seams.

Then came another much louder, unsuspected *BOOM* from the tank. This "boom" was louder than the original shots from Dad's rifle, but it was not as loud as we had anticipated, for the tank was still in one piece and we were all still alive.

This third mid-sized unsuspected boom had come from the sudden release of the expanding gases into the air. These gas fumes had been growing inside the tank at uncontrollable rates, as the heat of the fire was turning the liquid gas into expanding gas-fume particles.

The squealing hissing from the gunshot hole had ceased and was replaced by a noise that sounded like the blowing horn of a large ship. This rapid *BWH-BWH-BWH---* came from the top of the tank as the tank appeared to vibrate.

These gasses were escaping from a new-formed 3-inch hole in the top of the tank, where a screw-on fill-cap had once been. The fill-cap had burst off from the top of the tank, like a rocket fired upwards into the air, and the lid disappeared into the black clouds above. This 3-inch fill-cap had been on the top of the fuel tank to keep the rain and bugs out. The fill-cap could be unscrewed and removed so that a delivery-truck driver could fill the empty tank with new fuel.

This sudden release of built-up gasses, no doubt, saved the tank from most certain destruction and saved our lives, as well.

At this sign of hope, the neighbours kicked into high gear and began running wildly about, like a legion of organized army ants, with buckets of water and were putting out the remainder of this now-yielding fire.

They were yelling to each other, "This way men!" and "More bloody water, over here... More water, and by all means, man, hit the fire this time. That water went in my boots."

Other neighbours said to Nedge, who was running back and forth with a re-purposed cup of water that he was using for his bucket, "What are you doing here, kid? Go back to your mother. That cup of water ain't gonna help any. Scat, you little brat! Just look'at what'ya did."

As Nedge hung his head with defeat and a great measure of shame and regret, he choked back a tear. This went on until the fire was completely out, and, for a moment, there was a peaceful calm. Sweat was pouring down the faces of our neighbours, and tears were in the eyes of some as they thanked God for saving their lives from this brush with death. A near-brush with death will do this to any man or woman.

Then came the screaming sirens of the fire trucks, who were ready for some crazy, unbelievable action; but there was only a now-dying bonfire to swarm upon and a couple of small hot-spots.

Before leaving, the firemen were kind enough to cut Dad's new rubber boots off, which were now melted to his feet like cold concrete. They then kindly gave my folks the bill for their lifesaving services. The firemen said, "Elvis, I advise you to keep a close eye these fool-headed kids of yours."

As the last car lights left our yard that evening, I could hear Dad calmly say to Mom, "I think, I'm gonna need a new pair of rubber boots."

Weeks later, I found that fuel tank fill-cap lying a hundred yards away from where the tanks were, in some new-growing grass. I was so excited and proud to show Nedge my new-found treasure. We happily headed to show Dad our treasure as we puffed out our chests like proud peacocks in hope of redeeming ourselves... just in case Dad was still thinking of giving us up for adoption, or sending us to jail.

It is hard for some people to not look at you with disdain and suspicion for the rest of your life when you have made a small mistake, particularly when you have put their lives in grave danger, so redeeming ourselves was a critical objective to shake off the guilts.

Finding this cap was the needed hope that was the key to breaking off the chains of guilt that gripped our hearts for weeks after the fire. This cap brought some much-needed happiness to Nedge and myself as we showed Dad our new-found prize, like a grand trophy won for last place. Dad liked the treasure so much that he used it as his make-shift cigarette ashtray for many years after, to remind him that his boys had, certainly, inherited the McVanBuck fire-fool gene.

Chapter Four

****

Ketchup Graffiti

Joy and I just discovered the other morning that we, as parents, have a blossoming artist in our home. As I passed by the end of the hallway, something caught my attention. There were some very nice, classy red and blue ink lines which had appeared within the last ten minutes. These classy marker lines started about halfway up the wall and proceeded down the hall, into a bedroom, and around a corner where they suddenly disappeared into the closet behind some closed doors.

Silently, without a sound, I slid the closet door open and there I found my three year-old daughter, a young Picasso artist in the makings, sitting cross-legged on the floor, working hard on her latest artwork with her markers in hand. It is so hard to find such hard workers these days, good thing there is still some hope in the world.

Her baby doll lay in her lap. I had to do a double-take. The vibrant coloured lines of the hallway were now also covering her poor Dolly's head. There was a generous layer of red and blue lines encircling each of her Dolly's eyes.

The doll looked like a zombie from the underworld. Being a good dad means you have to use self-restraint when talking to young minds, so I didn't give voice to my inner feelings. My inner feelings were in a state of stunned shock, and when these feeling are in a state of shock, they tend to blurt out words that crush the motivation of hard workers. My thoughts were now restrained to what I truly thought about the new look on her dolly's face, as my little three-year old would not understand that her dolly looked like a beaten-up boxer with his face pounded black and blue from his opponent's gloves.

"Dolly needed some hair because she's bald, 'cause she's a girl, and she needs mommy's eye makeup," my daughter informed me, as she noticed me standing there speechless.

My voice was lacking a good response. It is hard to argue with the voice of reason; Mommy did over-do the make-up sometimes and that always left me speechless as well.

"Isn't she beautiful?" my daughter gushed with glee, glancing up at my face and then down again to Dolly's face.

Sputtering out a reply, I said, " 'Dolly' is now officially renamed 'Scribbles,' I would believe that to be a fitting new name. And from henceforth, artwork is restricted to paper only, my little angel."

I handed a wet rag to my daughter for her to learn that "cleanliness is next to godliness" and she set about trying to remove the artwork that she had drawn on the hallway wall. Her scrubbing only lasted five minutes before she disappeared.

My mind went back to some very bold, unique artwork that I had the privilege of seeing and experiencing first-hand as a kid, and I chuckled to myself.

It all started early one morning with my mom Becky's voice drifting down into my sleep and pulling me out from the depths of my sweet slumber. The stern, disapproving note of her voice could no longer be ignored, as she called for all five of her offspring to quickly make their appearance in the kitchen.

As I laid in the cocoon of my blankets, struggling to force my eyes open, suddenly Mom's voice boomed out directly over my head, "Wake Up!...Now, Mister!"

As her voice broke the quiet, the light in my room, simultaneously, flicked on and now burned the sleep from my eyes. I was forced out of bed by Mom and I stumbled to join my four other siblings who were already standing alert, shoulder-to-shoulder, trying to rub the sleep from their eyes. Their eyes also looked like they had been caught in the high-beam headlights of a car in the middle of the night. For this 6 a.m. wake-up call was way earlier than our normal morning 8 o'clock get-up time.

We were promptly asked with some unfriendly tones coming from Mom, her shoe tapping a frightening and disapproving tune, "Who did this?"

I was not sure which bad thing I had done the day before that she had now stumbled upon, or if it was one of my other siblings' works of destruction that she was talking about. I definitely got the impression that someone had done something... wrong.

One of us kids asked sweetly and

innocently, "Dear Mother, what are you talking about, my loving and sweet Mother... dear?!"

Mom yanked open the fridge door with an irritated jerking motion and said, "THIS!"

Once my eyes adjusted to the light coming out of the fridge as the door was flung open, I was shocked at the scene on the inside of the fridge, that met my eyes. I could assume that all of my other siblings felt the same way I felt, except for the evil villain among us who had done the deed, and now stood beside us.

For in the fridge, I could clearly see that something was out of harmony, besides the typical rotting head of lettuce that had now turned into slime, the half block of moldy cheddar cheese, and the sort.

With the busyness of farm life and Mom's need for a full fridge, the food in the fridge sometimes got left there a bit too long for my taste buds... but Mom liked her food ripe.

For Mom always said, "You kids are not going to go hungry like I did in my day," adding, "And I cannot trust the refrigeration at the grocery store, I can't see the refrigeration over there if I am home, now can I?"

Again, who could argue with the voice of reason? She was right, she could not see the food slowly rotting in the store refrigeration.

Now, the light was revealing a problem

that was not normally found within Mom's busy fridge. There was ketchup sprayed all over the contents of the fridge. There was ketchup on the cucumbers; ketchup on the milk jug. There was even ketchup on the ketchup bottle itself! This spraying of ketchup had been performed with the plastic ketchup squirt bottle. And from top to bottom, there were mad lines of ketchup everywhere, zigzagging this way and that.

It looked to me like it had been a lot of fun for the person who had done this bold act. Concealing this artwork on the inside of the fridge was definitely smart, but keeping it hid was most certainly short-lived. I must admit, I had had these very same urges to squirt the ketchup into the fridge come to my mind before, but I did not have the bravery to act upon these impulses, and, obviously, someone had beat me to it! It was apparent there was someone else who possessed another level of bravery inside of them. Those levels of bravery were hard steps to follow. One of us McVanBuck kids was going to be in big trouble.

I made the suggestion that maybe, somehow, there must be a logical explanation to the dripping, red ketchup mess that laid before us.

I said, "Maybe, by chance, the ketchup bottle got too hot in there and made an

KETCHUP

accidental explosion all on its own."

This suggestion drew suspicion as to me being the culprit, as well as unwanted glares from the entire family's eyeballs. I quickly and adamantly denied this, as I was drilled with questions and accusations. My siblings came at me like savage wolves and fired-off trick questions like good lawyers do, to trip up the criminal on the witness stand.

Words like, "AH-HA," and, "Eureka! We caught you red-handed, you little ketchup vandal!" came from my oldest sister, Zoey.

I tried to dodge direct-eye contact from their eyes of fire and brimstone. Mom had this eye-bulging stare that burned laser-holes deep into your soul and would make one confess to crimes you did not commit, so it was critical to avoid her eyes in particular.

We kids called this form of parental eye-torture, "the eye-boogle". Calvin, the youngest of us McVanBuck kids, once tried to counter this torturing technique by giving a solid eye-boogle of his own, back at Mom, but he had very limited success. At first, this had the desired affect as it brought shock and dismay to Mom... but this was short-lived when she doused his fiery flame with a counter-attack of the biggest eye-boogle I have ever seen. Calvin's face went pale and he was forced to stare at the floor. I figured this must have been his inner-self making him to look down, so that his soul could live another day inside his body. Mom's eyes had pretty much came right out of her head and stayed bulged out for a week, and Calvin was sent to run his twenty laps around the house as punishment, for the army would have no slackers and no countering eye-boogles from any of her soldiers.

Any form of discipline, new or old, I would not have liked at all in this very moment, for I was not the vandal... even if I had the thought of being a vandal at times, it did not make me the current vandal. For I was resisting the temptation of squirting the ketchup bottle with a great deal of inner self-control.

My defence drew little hope of being believed, and my case seemed all but lost, for true justice. When all seemed to be lost, my hero came to my aid, in the form of my brother Nedge.

His voice broke into the air and he spoke like a nervous little song bird, coming to my defence, "You know, maybe by chance... hmm... I did this?...like, you know, in my sleep?... like, you know, sleep walkers do... maybe?"

I suppose, that to him, this was a logical answer to the problem at hand. No one was ready to confess to this inner fridge art, and Nedge's confession was the hook that Mom was looking to bite upon. He was quickly marched outside to run twenty laps around the house; we could hear his wailing and baaing coming from outside, for he hated running laps.

He wheezed and said, "If I have to do one more lap, I will faint," as he started lap two of the task.

Things went back to normal for about a week; then the ketchup bandit struck the fridge again with the same ketchup ammo. Apparently, Mom had refilled the ketchup bottle because when I had given it a squirt at the inside of the fridge a couple of days earlier, to my disappointment, it had been empty. She must have filled the ketchup bottle back up after my copy-cat attempt. Luck was just not on my side due to the high competition in our home and my bad timing.

Nedge immediately became the prime suspect this time, as we all once again stood there in-line, scorning him with our eyes, our arms crossed in a disapproving manner. But Nedge was certain that he did not do this act of sleep-walking vandalism, because, as he told Mom, he had been sleeping with one eye open recently. He had been keeping that eye open, to catch the true ketchup bandit that was striking the fridge at night.

Nedge was seriously getting into the part of a convincing child actor, for he was really starting to sound believable through all of his filthy lies. I was seriously impressed with his lying abilities. I thought, *he could become a politician or even fake the moon landing of an astronaut with his believable lying skills.*

At the moment that he was about to be marched outside for a second stint of running twenty laps, my sister Daisy, who was a year older than myself, spoke up after a long, awkward silence, "I think I may have done it... but it was truly an accident... it really was an accident... both times," her lips quivering.

I suppose she could not bear another week of guilt for her really big "accidents".

With horror written all over her face, Mom sharply asked Daisy, "So it was you who squirted the fridge with ketchup!?! The first time as well?!?"

Daisy stammered, "Well... yes, it was me... but... but accidents happen."

Daisy never became a famous artist, with her blossoming artistic abilities being quenched early with the huffings and wheezings of running fifty laps. Some people just do not make the grade for becoming a good actor or artist. And she was one of them, she could not keep straight paint lines on a canvas no matter how hard she tried.

Afterwards, I tried comforting Daisy a little by saying, "It's just one of the drawbacks of being in the house with a lot of very smart people."

This was the last we saw of the ketchup bandit's handiwork; the ketchup bandit never struck again. The would-be copy-cat bandit never struck either, for seeing Daisy clean up the ketchup off of everything in the fridge and running the fifty laps did not look like much fun at all to me.

Chapter Five

⁂

Thistle Attack

In recent years, the dog ticks have moved into my area of Canada, and have been multiplying in vast numbers. These insects thrive in long grasses when they are young. When ticks grow up a little, they get bored of their surroundings, because their new wives make them mow the grass twice a week, and they decide, at that point, to go on tour to escape the yard work. They do this by jumping onto the backs of humans and furry mammals, much like a gang of stowaway hobos on a train.

As Tick Billy's wife screeches at him to get out and start mowing again, Tick Billy yells over the hedge to his next-door neighbour, from his poverty-stricken sod house, "Hey, Sammy? Let's blow this neighbourhood, and go on vacation. I hate mowing the lawn."

"Yeah, let's get out of here, before I have to vacuum the grassy carpet! But where will we go?" Sammy the Sucker whines back.

Tick Billy responds, "I don't know. Hey, look here! Get on this here dog, quick. We can hitch a ride on him."

Ticks are lazy and are poor planners for long road trips, so it isn't long before Sammy the Sucker is griping and complaining again, "Boy, am I thirsty, my lips are sure parched and my canteen's plum empty."

Tick Billy calls over, as he shrugs his eight shoulders, "Hey, why don't you just suck the blood of this here mammal that we're riding?

Sammy the Sucker enthusiastically replies, "Oh boy, that sounds delicious! Too bad we left in such a hurry, I forgot my fork and knife. I'll have to just suck him dry with my gums."

Where the ticks lack in work ethic, they make up in their ability to adjust to rapid change. I guess there is no shortage of blood to go around for these nasty little parasites.

It's just not all that pleasant of a sight to find one of those unclean hobos clinging onto one of my children, robbing a blood transfusion at my child's expense. The ticks don't even offer to pay for the meal, except for maybe in the way of giving them lime's disease as an unwanted tip.

In one small case my wife, Joy, found one of their sneaky little feeding grounds. She was trying to get cuddled up with me one evening at bedtime just before turning the nightlight off.

She started to lean her peaceful head onto my arm, to snuggle on it, and make it her pillow for the night. This is when her eyes unexpectedly saw an unwanted guest invading my personal space.

Without warning, she promptly went into testing my hearing with a deadly, shrill *"Eeeeeeeeewww!"* The high-pitched scream combed the hair down on the back of my head, and my ears flattened to my skull. This paralyzing sound was just a tweak shy of breaking my eardrums.

Her high-pitched scream was excessive, and my ears are still ringing to this day. This proved to me that her lips were way too close to my ears. Those terrifying screeches are only meant to be heard from down inside the hole to the underworld. Joy's bulging eyes were also down-right impressive. She leapt right out of bed like a spooked cat and jumped over the top of the lamp. This was all done in one spectacular movement. Her leap was pretty close to Jack's amazing jump over the candle stick, as she easily cleared the top of the lamp.

This put me into a paralyzed, stunned state-of-mind at first, like I had been stung by a deadly jellyfish. As I tried to clean out the ringing in my ear with my baby finger, I thought, *If it's the Grim Reaper coming for us, I'm going to be a goner for sure.* With my lack of hearing, I would be no good at hearing the Grim Reaper's eerie, "W-O-o... W-O-o," if there was any.

This was what I imagined... until I saw what had made Joy scream and jump about. Her protruding eyes, out-stretched arm, and wiggling finger were now pointing at the fearful sight from the other side of the room. Her other hand, she held over her mouth. I thought it was a little late to be covering her mouth now, but it was the loving thought that counted... yet it was not going to help bring back any of my hearing.

When my eyes locked onto the blood-sucking beast, that she was making all of the fuss about, I then made my own motivated moves. Unfortunately, all of the screaming, leaping, and running laps around the bedroom was not helping. The feasting tick, in my mildly toxic armpit, did not even budge from his meal. He was, apparently, yawning with boredom, even with my wild running and arms flailing like a dancing orangutan. This tick did not even bother to take his deeply buried, blood-sucking head out for a moment, which a retract-and-retreat action on his part would have been more than welcome.

The tick must have been mighty thirsty to be having a midnight snack in my armpit. At least, this I could assume from its fat backside and smacking lips. Joy refused to get within ten feet of helping me remove it. It seemed that the next step for her would be to go into shell-shock, grab her knees, and cry for her mommy. I'd have to terminate this tick's rental agreement, for being a squatter, on my own. So I heartlessly executed him for his crimes of gluttony, hole-punching, violating private property, being a sickening menace, and a number of other lesser violations of the human armpit.

When these ticks moved into our area, apparently, I was one of the first people to have noticed that these unwanted guests had arrived.

So when my elderly neighbour, Mr. Brown, came to visit one day, he was quite adamant that, "There are no ticks in Central Saskatchewan. You must be mad," because of his vast local knowledge of 90-plus years of living in the same area. "Yer an ignorant outsider because you lived in British Columbia! It's too cold out here fer ticks! I've been here for ninety years. There is no ticks. Yer thinking of fleas. Now, now, Saskatchewan has lots of fleas, of course, but not ticks... ouch! You little bugger... ouch!" he exclaimed, as he scratched the back of his neck; and three or four fleas went jumping this way and that.

The only fleas that I had seen in this part of the country were located on the sole-breeding ground of Mr. Brown's own wrinkly body, giving the fleas plenty of hiding spots to multiply in. It's a good thing I have learned to cover the mouth of my coffee cup with my hand, to protect it from incoming shrapnel, while visiting with Mr. Brown. The in-coming jumping fleas bounced off the back of my hand because of my quick reflexes. These reflexes saved the fleas from a hot bath. On the other hand, Mr. Brown could have used a hot bath. But, then again, a bath would have turned his bathwater blacker than the coffee in my cup. Truth be told, I would have done a poor job of straining out those fleas from my coffee with my teeth, like Mr. Brown did, due to having one front tooth missing, making my teeth a very poor coffee strainer.

The fact was, Mr. Brown had hardly driven

further than a ten-mile radius of his farm in some ninety years, and yet he was calling me the ignorant outsider to the ways of Saskatchewan. I was, evidently, still an outsider, because I had been living in Saskatchewan in the same house for only ten years, after moving in from Northern British Colombia. But it is hard to argue with a local fossil like Mr. Brown.

When people get older, sometimes it's extremely difficult to try to reason with them that life, in fact, does change. With old-age comes the unwanted moles and skin tags -- just like the one that was growing on the top of Mr. Brown's head -- and there was also the moustache that was growing out of his ears. These were changes that Mr. Brown, apparently, wasn't aware of.

It is that stubborn streak that can only be taught one way; with actual proof, evidence, and another ten local farmers as witnesses to the actual event, testifying that the event had really happened. Then it could be, indeed, classified as an "event change".

Now, up to this point, I was never aware that Mr. Brown ever had one of those large skin tags on the top of his head, and this one was quite big for a skin tag, perhaps the size of a pea. It's one of those odd things in life, that when you are looking at something brand new growing on somebody's face, such as new hair sprouting out of their ears, that your eyes just stare at it. They are drawn to the new thing by some sort of higher, secret magnetic force that is beyond the eyes' control, like a lower form of hypnotism!

At this point in time, you just try to pretend that everything is perfectly normal, and you attempt to not stare at the new growing beauty marks for too long. Seemingly, prolonged staring is perceived as rude, but to the gawker, it's just shock.

So you look at the "THING" briefly, then dart your eyes away; you look at the "THING" again, just to make sure that your eyes are not playing tricks on you, then you dart your eyes away, once more, from the THING"that is pulling on your eyes. It's also wise to rest your knuckles under your chin, as this will keep your mouth from falling open at the sight of the THING" in question. This is what we call "being polite," but I'm only guessing here, because I never went to a polite finishing school. Although, I'm sure I would fit in perfectly well with the polished people.

The longer I talked with Mr. Brown, the more stubborn he became, as I tried to bring some kind of sanity and straight thinking to his stubbornness. He looked at me like I was some sort of lying parasite, myself, who was sucking out his thoughts and pulling him into a wild story of deceit.

The more I dug in, building up my case that ticks were in our area and truly existed locally, the more stubborn and adamant he became that there were no ticks -- even to the point that he appeared to be getting angry with a glowing-red face.

He pounded his hand on the table as he started to rise off of his chair, insisting, "There's no ticks in Saskatchewan!"

Even after telling Mr. Brown the story of my first-hand sighting of the unsightly beast, that had made residence in my armpit, I could not persuade the old hairy-eared geezer; even when I gave him a simple example of things changing, like the fact that he had hair growing out of his ears... and wasn't that a change?

He simply replied by saying, "I've always had hair growin' outta my ears."

I questioned him with shock in my voice, "You had hair growing in your ears, even when you were a baby?"

He replied, "Why yes, I did. Hmm...mmm, I was an early bloomer -- back in the day!" I might add that Mr. Brown said this rather proudly, like it was a badge of hairy honour.

I do have to say, that as a kid, he would have been the child with the most hair growing out of his ears. Maybe he even had hair growing out of his ears as a baby, but we

call those types of babies werewolves, nowadays. For it's most assuredly a werewolf, when a comb is needed to untangle the hair that is mysteriously coming out of one's ears.

There was this other experience that I had, which again, when telling Mr. Brown the story in trying to make him believe my encounters with these insects, his stubborn streak would not allow him to accept change that involved his life and his surrounding environment.

I had run into these tick parasites when I had been working as a heavy equipment operator, grading the Saskatchewan prairie roads, for that was my trade at the time.

I needed to make a pit stop, to go to the washroom. Now, if it is the typical relieving myself of the two gallons of water, that is no big deal. This secret is just done beside the heavy-equipment road grader, when no one is looking. If it is an event of where I need to relieve myself of my wife's cooking from the night before, that is going to need a bit more of a private location. In this case, the private location, out in the countryside, was a vacant, abandoned homestead. The land around this homestead had been gobbled up by one of the larger farm operations, and the yard went quiet with no people around.

The yard site had been unkempt for some

years. It now grew tall grass, wild weeds, wicked Canadian thistles, an array of Bull thistles, like large purple-flowered plums sprinkled about, as well as some nasty, evil bur weeds known as Burdock Arctium.

The Dutch use these weeds as herbs for many ailments, such as a scalp treatment to fix the itch, I believe, or was it to fix the flakes? Those Dutch go hardcore with their bur-weed oil. But I have found the only good use for these burs, is to use them as a cure for the ailment called laziness. For whenever I get wandering into a patch of burs in error, I end up with ten thousand unwanted prickly burs in my clothes, and I am stuck with them until I pick them off -- one by one -- for the next two hours!

Looking for a good spot to relieve myself, I decided to deposit the load at the far corner of the vacant homestead. I wove my way carefully around the thistles and past the Burdock burs. Seeing a good-sized red ant hill, I paused a moment, to give it some good kicks with my boot, to get them livened up and give them something to do. Then I carried on and avoided a large wasp-nest home, which was built in an abandoned badger hole in the ground. The wasp nest was about the size of a basketball, and I resisted the urge to give this hive a kick.

Finally, I found my perfect hiding spot

behind a clump of tall trees. I dropped my trousers and work coveralls to my ankles, in a very common human-type fashion, and set out to get this business out of the way, before it made an appearance in an unwanted way, in my wife's laundry, like a stray brown cat running across the lawn.

As my ‘business’ drew to a conclusion, I looked down at the inside of my drawers and made a frightening discovery -- that thankfully was no brown cat. Apparently, I had ran headlong into a nest of dog ticks, for there was not just one tick crawling around inside my drawers, but a whole army of ticks. The ticks were there as if they had just found new territory and had conquered it by just showing up, uninvited. There were far too many ticks to count at a quick glance, and this army was multiplying by the microsecond, as they climbed off the surrounding tall grass and into my sunken pair of trousers and underpants!

The next procedure was that, I needed to make a choice. There were too many ticks to just pick them off, one by one, for who knew how many new ticks would climb aboard, like a gang of hobos onto my clothing from the tall grass, if I had tried removing one tick at a time.

It was at this moment that the words of my fourth-grade teacher came to mind. She would say to me, "Peter, you are going to do your math now or you will be going to jail!" ...it went something like that.

Boy, she was right. I didn't want to go to jail, so I learned math fast, and it sure came in handy at this time. So in my head, with the help of my fingers and my toes, I quickly calculated that while I picked one tick off, I would have at least two or three more ticks climbing aboard, into my clothing. And apparently, this was a very large dog-tick family which, obviously, had all twins and triplets for children, because they were all identically, very ugly kids.

With this horror unfolding in front of me, a split-second decision needed to be made. I decided that I needed to get to the grader as quickly as humanly possible to get these hobo-riding ticks off of me. The lump of new soil, laying on the grass behind me, was also a highly-motivating factor to vacate the premises quickly.

Now the grader was parked some hundred metres away, and what laid between me and the grader was nothing but that tall grass, those thistles, and the weeds. Taking off my pant-ware, shoes, and clothes and then running naked through the grass wasn't an option, with the thistles and burs in the way. Pulling up my pants and drawers with a hobo clan of ticks inside, was most certainly not an option, either!

With a firm decision needing to be made quickly, the only logical option remaining was to bunny-hop my way out of this mess. So I started hopping, as if in a potato sack race. It was the greatest race of all time, with maximum speeds and high jumps being my main focus. I was hoping that, with some luck, I could shake off some of the clinging ticks with the wind that was blowing between my legs, or bounce the ticks off with the shock waves of my feet hitting the ground.

These spirited leaps were aided by an inner fear, which had the intensity of an ancient Egyptian nine-tailed whip on my back! Being a slave to the fear of an insect slowly sucking your blood will really get a person moving an extra knot or two faster.

Danger seemed to be everywhere, as I tried to dodge the thistles with my wild frantic jumps, going this way and that. It seemed that the zigzagging helped me to get away from a small patch of purple Bull thistles and burs, but instead it led me into much larger patches of Canadian thistles. Instead of jumping over the thistles, which I had calculated in my head would be quite easy to do, with my quick math, I jumped right into the thistle patch. Perhaps my math was wrong, this would have worked if my jumps were a little bigger and the thistle and bur plants a little shorter than their five-foot height. Looking back, only in my mind could I have made those leaps, but fate would not allow mind over matter in this healthy patch of thriving thistles.

It would have also helped if I could've been able to pull my pants back up to my waist, to enable me to make such good-sized jumps, but with my clothing-shackled feet, my jumping was in vain. Heightened anxiety and fear are deceptive in making you believe you can do more than the moon jumps of an astronaut. But fear can only take a person so high into the air. Even if the mind is telling you, "Higher, I said HIGHER," you are not going to jump like a spooked white-tailed deer just like that, no matter how high the fear level is, or how many thistles and burs are accumulating inside your pants, which are still shackled around your feet like a giant tumbleweed.

With this maddening dash, thankfully, there weren't any spectators, who usually show up at times like this, to clock my world-record speed in the potato sack race though the thistle and bur patches. When the jumping attempts over the thistles and Burdock burs failed with each "Ouch, oh, ah, eck, ouch," I just decided to wing-it and make a shortcut straight through the thistle patch with the biggest jump I could muster. I envisioned this jump would be as high as an Olympic pole-vaulter, just without the pole or the Olympic-sized skill-level to go with it.

This is when I found the badger hole with both of my feet, as I landed in it. I had not been able see the badger hole with my eyes, due to the height of the thistles obstructing my view. This is when panic bolted past fear, as my memory kicked in, for it was reminding me that there was a large grey paper wasp nest in the hole that I was now standing in. The wasp nest was now a deflated basketball under my feet, and my trousers were still hanging at my ankles.

My boots were stuck in the badger hole like wet concrete. Wasps, it seems, do not like having the gates of their city kicked in. It was apparent that this hive of wasps were also easily provoked when I started swatting at them with my full toilet-paper roll while stomping up and down on their nest, as I tried to free my feet from the grip of the badger hole.

Using the toilet-paper roll in my hand like a medieval war mace was some quick thinking, but did little good in beating the attackers off. This wild whacking at the ticks and wasps with my homemade soft mace was like the soft blows of a pillow and only seemed to provoke them more, like poking at a mean dog who had rabies with a stick.

The ticks that had climbed aboard the inside my clothing, also seemed to be as terrified of the wasps as I was, for the ticks were starting to climb up my legs for the safety of higher grounds. But those higher grounds were way-off limits for them, in my mind! My mind was numb with fear, but not blind to madness!

As the wasps zoomed around with rage, my legs were easy targets for them to sting, and with the invading army of ticks from beneath, this gave me the needed incentive to take a temporary loss.

So I flopped onto my backside into the thistles and burs, and army rolled out of harm's way. This worked brilliantly in freeing my feet from the badger hole, and I wormed myself speedily away from the swarm of wasps. The speed of my worm crawl would have been impressive if I had been a snake fleeing its natural enemy, but for a human with only bare skin as a shield against the thistle-riddled, rocky soil; this is called "madness". When my body could not take any more of the grating upon the skin, I stopped to catch my breath and get back on my feet, but not before I noticed that I had inadvertently crawled onto the aggravated ant hill that had been flattened by my boot when I had entered the homestead.

This spot was a poor location to lose all the

wind in my sails. The ants were no ally either, in fact, they had a great deal of fierceness to their biting. It was as if they had abandon all compassion and lost their minds, as they started biting me while they all rushed to climb aboard. The ants' burning bites only added to my torments of pain, and I began to feel a bit of regret for bulldozing their sky-rise. I fought them off the best I could, as I tried to get my feet back under me to jump to safety out of this nightmare. As my feet got relocated back under me, I was able to get some momentum in my jumps. With the swarm of wasps hot on my trail around my head again (for they did not forget the act of war against their city very easily), and the armies of ticks and ants invading from the south -- which were getting far too close to my private property -- I was feeling that impending mortal dome was nigh.

Once I hit the gravel road, safety was within reach. My scratched body was speckled with biting and stinging insects which left large welts, making me look like I had just caught a bad case of the chickenpox; but I was gold. I climbed into the cab of the grader, closed the door to the air assault of the wasps, and quickly removed all of my clothes down to my birthday suit.

Then for the next two hours, I went through the painfully slow process of removing each and every one of these ticks, ants, and wasps still clinging tightly to the inside of my clothes and legs without being stung or bit any more than necessary. It was also a real treat to avoid being pricked by the thistles and burs that were sticking to my clothes.

There was this thought of just leaving all of my clothes right there on the side of the road, and just lighting a match to burn the whole pile of clothes in a McVanBuck fashion, for they were tangled with thistles, burs, and insects beyond recognition. But burning my clothes was just not a sensible option for this situation. I was not going to show up that evening at the workshop, driving a piece of heavy equipment with nothing on, but a sheepish grin.

-- After I had shared this first-hand experience with Mr. Brown, that made me very much certain and aware that ticks, in fact, were in our area; he scoffed all the more. I also could've told Mr. Brown that the Bull thistles, Burdock burs, badgers, wasps and red ants were thriving; but he would not have believed that either. Like a stubborn old farmer, Mr. Brown could not be convinced, even though he could clearly see the good number of welts on my face and hands.

Laughing and mocking, he said, "That's flea-a-a bites on your face and neck, you fool! ...sees, here I got's them all over here meself!" And he showed me the four red welted spots that ran down the side his neck. He then got up from the table and headed to his car to go back to his farm, still laughing as he went and shaking his head as fleas jumped this way and that.

It was at this point, I turned to Joy and said, "My goodness! Did you see the size of that tick that's latched onto the top of his head? It's as big as the tip of my thumb -- looks like an old man's skin tag! I would a-reckon that tick has been sucking on Mr. Brown's old-man blood for days. That tick's stuffed itself full and is ready to relocate, is my guess."

Joy replied, "And did you see the smaller tick on his ear?" She then made a little, *"ugh"* gagging sound and a noticeable shiver went up her spine.

I responded, "At least, he'll have his own 'tick-proof evidence' the next time we see him."

A week later, Mr. Brown was back. This time, his eyes were wide-open and were as big as the hubcaps on a car. He was trying to convince me, now, that we people in Saskatchewan have a tick invasion in our area!

Oh, what a surprise, I thought to myself!

He acted like he hadn't heard a word of truth about my experiences with these unwanted spongers, the last time we had talked to him. Mr. Brown must have had quite the tale to tell the local people, as he gossiped around the neighbourhood from house to house telling of "his" wild stories, because within days, I was hearing my own tick stories coming back to me.

My only question was, when that tick which was latched onto the top of his head had grown to its maximum size, filled with Mr. Brown's blood -- did it really plop into his bowl of soup that he was having for dinner, or was Mr. Brown just telling us a wild story?

Chapter Six

⁂⁂

Rat Invaders

There are leaders in this world and there are followers. My good neighbour Mr. Brown, most certainly, is a follower, but he is somehow not aware of this fact. I do find that a lot of people are followers. That's kind of normal. The top five percent of people in this world are leaders, and the other ninety-five percent pretend to be leading. So, much like my tick story, unless Mr. Brown experienced something first-hand, like something swimming around in his soup, he wasn't going to pay attention to me, the follower.

There are also other pest invaders which are high on the hatred list of a good many farmers. The prairies are well-known for the mass invasions of prairie gophers that wreak havoc on ranch land with their relentless compulsion to dig yet another hole, to add to their collection of thirty other holes. It's like they have some crazed addiction to digging. These holes create many problems for horses, cows, and sheep who step into these holes and break their legs off.

Another invader is the army worm, which is a black furry caterpillar, about the size of your finger. These army worms munch down on a canola crop with devastating results, as I saw first-hand as a kid. I would wake up in the middle of the night with nightmares that a million army worms were out to get me and were in my hair, wiggling around. It is just an ugly image that is hard to shake out of a young mind.

Now, rats were the most recent type of plague, which I had never seen before. In my younger years while growing up, in the province of Alberta, Canada, which has a very unique eradication program to this day, I had never seen a rat. It is the only jurisdiction in North America that has no rats. Honestly, no rats at all! If one live rat is found, an eradication unit consisting of a small army of rat killers is sent to find, identify, and then destroy them all.

So if you have a pet shop in an Albertan town, and you have rats in cages to feed your snakes, reptiles, and other pets, then you had best keep you eyes open for the Albertan rat patrol.

The rat patrol are easy to spot, for they have a club in one hand and a bucket of poison in the other, and, if you look closely, you will see a rat trap in each of their pockets, just waiting for one of your rats to get loose so they can prove to the government of Alberta, that they are effectively doing their job. This only make sense -- for it's easier to just find a rat in your local pet shop than to find one that is running loose in a farmer's open field.

So, me being the natural-born leader, pretender or otherwise, it was only natural for the rats to attack my Saskatchewan farm first. It was inevitable. Like any wise opposing army, they would attack the leaders first, then work their way down the ranks.

Now, the first time in my life that I saw rats, was in my chicken coop. We have hens on our country place and they lay eggs. Hens are a wonderful bird. They give you an egg and a cackle in the morning, as they are happy to lay that egg for the farmer each day. But when I go out to the outhouse to lay my egg, I am not cackling because I am happy, I am cackling because of the lack of fibre and prunes.

The other day I asked my daughter, "Is that hen cackling because she's so happy to have an egg each morning?"

Her reply was, "Definitely, because all the other hens attack and peck her head from sheer jealousy."

I have to agree with my daughter because that particular hen does not have a feather left on her head. The rest of the hens go after her with a mob mentality, with focus and vision, as soon as she successfully squirts out an egg with a cackle, but instead of a lynching, she gets plucked. This hen must be my highest producer of eggs. She is bald, not because she's old, but because she is blessed. I know that she knows that she is blessed, for she is happy to take the flurry of peckings from the other hens.

God should be praised for His creativity and dual-purpose creatures; for He created eggs, meat, and manure to come out of the same creature. The chicken is a really cool creature. My wife wanted to inform me that fresh chicken manure, though good for the garden outside, is somehow not very good for the plants in her bay window, and is extremely toxic to her nose. When she said she needed some manure for the plants in her house, apparently, there is a difference between fresh manure and decomposed manure.

All these house rules to proper plant fertilization make my head spin and my hands stink, but there is no point getting married unless you are willing to deal with a lady and her house plants.

One morning, when I went out to collect the daily eggs in our chicken coop, that our balding brown-coloured chickens had laid, I got an unpleasant surprise. I opened the door and there were two black Norway rats sitting in the chicken nesting boxes, which were located about four feet off of the ground. Now, if you catch this particular type of rat by surprise, it is like catching a homeless man in your bathtub.

They give you that look of, “Oh, no. This is embarrassing.” In the rats’ beady little eyes, I could see the intelligence of these vile beasts. Though rats are small, they are obnoxiously evil at their hearts. You could see in the one rat's eyes, the one that I would call the Einstein of the two, and in the way that his rat head darted back and forth, that he was calculating precise, mathematical equations of time, distance, and angles. He looked to be figuring out, how, in an emergency, he might need to run up my pant-leg and start to gnaw viciously on my knee, like a rabid woodpecker on a tree. This would be to bring a measure of distraction to me, the farmer. This type of distraction would, most certainly, be effective in forcing the farmer to drop his weapon of choice in horror and to start screaming, while beating the wiggling rat that was in his pant-leg with his fists.

Of course, this didn't happen; but the brain of a human tells you, that if that rat ever did get up inside your pant-leg and start chomping with those teeth, that this may indeed be a nightmare. As for the rat, fight is the last resort when it feels cornered; to fight would give the rat the needed moment to escape death in his desperation for survival.

McVanBuck Call of The Lighter

The other rat, the dumber one, I named Lewis, well, because he looked like a Lewis. Anyway, this burglar Lewis had an egg firmly grasped in his arms like a large football. He had his tongue sticking out the side of his little whiskered mouth, off to the left of his two yellowed buck teeth.

Now, Lewis the rat, did not seem to be on-the-ball, and it did not appear that he wanted to let go of that egg very willingly. My assumption was that he was going to carry that egg into his hole, in the chicken coop wall, for a 6-point touchdown. It looked like I was going to have to hand-tackle him to remove that egg from his dirty paws. Where Lewis had one up on me with deception, I could maybe beat him with my wits and snatch him with a fast pair of hands.

So as the smart rat, Einstein, leapt through the air, over a two-foot gap, down the chicken coop nesting box, and into his end-zone hole; the dumb rat Lewis just stared at me with his beady eyes until I went for him. And like in all good football games, there is always that guy that makes the blunder, and Lewis dropped the egg like a coward and ran for his hole. I grabbed a stick, which I had collected while the rat was in his stunned, muddled frame of mind and greed. I went for him, but missed by only two inches. I would've nailed him with that stick or crushed him in my left hand if he went towards that hand.

Joy told me later that crushing a rat in your hand is not that easy, especially if the rat is biting that hand in return. She had a point – a biting rat would be unpleasant. It possibly could give me some real pain and the black plague.

What really perplexed me, though, was just how the rats planned on removing those eggs from the nesting boxes, but I am positive it would have been an extremely special piece of intelligence. I know that if I had left Einstein for a few more minutes, he would have come out of his hole with baling twine, pulleys, makeshift egg-nets, and the works, to get that egg out.

I think that Lewis, on the other hand, was just going to chuck the egg over the edge of the egg box and hope for the best. If the egg broke there, four feet below on the chicken coop floor, even though Lewis would get scolded by Einstein, I am sure they would have worked out their differences and ate the egg right there. If the egg survived the fall, it would be up to Einstein to roll the egg into their hole, crack it open in their kitchen, and fry it on their little rat frying pan. Some smouldering, dry chicken manure would probably be used as their fuel.

To get the fire started, Lewis would be given the task of chewing on my electrical wiring in the chicken coop wall to hot-wire a spark or two and get a fire blazing. This would have explained his slowness, the goofy look on his face, his blistered tongue hanging out, and the scorched whisker tips on his cheeks.

It was apparent that these rats were the culprits to the disappearing eggs, that I had noticed had been going missing for several weeks.

So with the sighting of the two rats, I knew I had a rat invasion. The prairie farmer's rule is: if you see one rat, there is ten that you didn't see. And since I saw two rats, one smart and one that was mentally below-average for a rat, this would mean, with my calculations, that we would have exactly eleven rats, twelve if you counted their mama who I called The Big Bertha.

My first step was to get an assortment of wooden traps. These were beauties. They were like mouse traps, but super-sized! They hurt your fingers much more than a mouse trap, especially when they slam down on your hand, as you're blindly digging for that egg in the nesting box and you forgot where you put all of the set rat traps.

A sting like that always seems to hurt more when it catches you by surprise -- because you are not expecting the sting, like you would be if you stuck your fingers in the trap deliberately. So, for some weird reason, you whip your hand into the air, stare at it, grab your wrist, and just start shaking your hand in an attempt to just "shake it off". The other instinctive response would be to comfort your fingers by putting them into your mouth, but with a rat trap attached to your fingers, this makes it difficult to get them in. Now all the cackling, that is coming out of your mouth (unless there is a rat trap stuck in it), creates a stampede of hens heading your way to pluck your head bald as well.

If sticking your fingers in the trap is done on purpose, you simply would calmly say,

"Ouch! Oh, that is unpleasant, just like I suspected!" You would then calmly go for the trap first, without all the shaking and cackling. If you were unable to hold in all the cackles after the trap clamped down on your hand, at least you would be able to see the stampede of hens coming, before they started jumping on your head.

In the first week, after sighting Einstein and Lewis, I had killed twelve rats and lost four traps. The lost traps simply just went missing. I think this was due to the intelligence of the Einstein rat. This also, to my calculations, was telling me that there was more than the assumed twelve rats. I was going to need something with a little more bite to it. So I went to the local store and bought one kilo box of rat poison. The first night, I excitedly put a handful of rat poison out. I even put up a little sign saying, "Welcome: Gift for Einstein, eat up, yum, yum."

In the morning, the whole handful of poison was gone, and my little "Welcome" sign for Einstein was also missing. I assumed he was going to use my paper "Welcome" sign as his toilet-paper in his outhouse -- just to mock me, for he left some good-sized droppings behind.

So I put out two handfuls of poison for the following night. In the morning, the two handfuls of poison were missing and presumed eaten. So on the third day, I shook two more handfuls out of the box. But instead of putting away the remaining three-fourths of the box back up on the shelf, where I had been putting it for the past two nights, I simply laid the box of rat poison on its side beside the other two fresh piles of poison.

In the morning, to my amazement, the two piles were missing as well as the entire box of poison. The only thing left was the bottom corner of the cardboard box the poison had been in.

It is at that moment where you say, "Oohh, there's a lot of rats! There is not just two rats. This is a BIG rat invasion!" It was time to call in the Saskatchewan Rat Patrol.

Now, the Rat Patrol here in Saskatchewan, is a little different. Their intentions are simply to minimize the billions of dollars of lost economic growth done to crops and buildings, due to this plague called rats. So with a phone call, they arrived the next day with a 5-gallon bucket full of rat poison.

Within the week, the poison was all gone. So Rat Patrol gave me another bucket-full and that also vanished. The rat poison stopped disappearing about halfway through the third 5-gallon bucket of poison, and for this I was grateful because the rats were starting to really lay some damage to my buildings around the yard. Some of the buildings lost a good two feet off the bottom of the entire building, and I had to duck my head while going through the doorways to get through without clunking the top of my head. Rats can chew a hole straight through a 2x4 board and not even think twice. Around that time when I was heavily poisoning the rats, I saw rat holes in thin metal sheets as well as copper wires chewed in half with a rat laying beside the wire,and his tongue hanging out. When the poison didn't get that rat, his own lack of electrical intelligence cost Lewis his life.

So with my first-hand information in hand, I told Mr. Brown about the rats. All he did was laugh and scoff at me, "Harr, harr, harr! You don't know what yer talking about. We haven't seen rats in our area for many years!

And I've lived in the same spot fer ninety years!" With that he left, laughing and shaking his head at my crazy story, once again.

Just like clockwork, a week later Mr. Brown was there at my door to tell me some new information and news about the area. The rat invasions were back! When he had returned home, the previous week, he got to wondering if there really were rats around. It came to his mind that every day for months, whenever he was working beside his grain bin, he could hear something scratching and rustling inside of the grain bin. He had just assumed it was a bird that had gotten in through the hole in the roof, and was flying around inside the bin.

Now Mr. Brown thought that perhaps he should take a little peak inside of his grain bin. When he swung open the bin door, where he should have seen two thousand bushels of nice golden grain, he only saw a two-foot thick layer of scurrying black rats. The rats were all scrambling for their lives, trying to get away from the light, which was coming through the open door and piercing their eyes.

The sight of so many rats in one place, which just so happened to be in his valued grain bin, brought a great deal of shock and dismay to Mr. Brown. His mouth dropped open to the toes of his boots below, and with bewilderment on his ghostly-pale face, he just slowly closed the door behind him. What else could he do? So he just walked away.

Mr. Brown's words were, "No point in cryin' at my ten-thousand dollar loss, *wheeze,* at least the rats seemed happy, *wheeze*... In fact, I'd say they looked down right jolly. At that point, I thought that I might as well just let'em alone to finish off the last hundred bushels of grain in the bin, *wheeze.*" He sipped on our coffee with a much sadder face than normal, like he was sick with the flu.

I could have sworn that he was trying to choke back some tears, but what do I know? Mr. Brown is a very generous fellow to God's little creatures. And at least, Mr. Brown wouldn't have to sweep out any of the grain. I am not sure what he intended to do with that foot-thick pile of rat manure at the bottom of his granary, but I am sure he could talk to my wife for she has some plants in need of some manure. On the bright side, this manure would be in a small and manageable pellet form.

So with Mr. Brown's leading information, I truly understood that the rats were, indeed, coming from his rat-breeding sanctuary. A happy bunch of rats they must have been, for, obviously, he truly was the natural-born leader.

Chapter Seven

⁂*⁂

Smoking Toothpicks

It was not all that many years ago that most people smoked tobacco, both men and women. People smoked almost everywhere; in cars, in restaurants, in airplanes, in bed, and even on the toilet! There was never a moment to be lost. This was common place in the 1980's and smokers ruled the day. Everyone else had to hold their breath for the eight-hour plane flight.

When my mom Becky finally quit smoking

by her own free will, I was truly glad she could do it on her own strength without even my help, for my two younger brothers and I were less than equipped for the battle at hand. I have to say, though, I think that we three young sons added a special element of surprise, shock, and fear to our two smoking parents, in our quest to see if we could help them kick their habit of smoking cigarettes.

One day, in our public school in the mid 1980's, we found out the truth about smoking. The school was really pushing the "Smoking Is Bad For The Lungs" campaign. The teachers of our classes showed us some really scary photos of crusted black lungs from some dead guy. He had been a smoker, and he was now dead because of it. We could at least put one and one together, at that age, to figure out that smoking meant most certain death.

Our teachers instructed the students to drive home the "Smoking Is Bad For The Lungs" message wherever possible. The lung donor of the very scary lungs would have been so proud of his donation to science. He would have been especially proud to see the new heightened response of an army of kids thrust into action by nothing more than sheer fear and terror, being used at maximum efficiency. We all figured that we were going to be dead and dying of lung cancer by the time we hit grade six, and that our parents would be dead by the end of the week.

Miss Jackson said to us naive children, in her deep raspy voice with a cough, "Now you children, don't go out there and start smoking, OK? You can clearly see what this evil habit will most assuredly do to you, *hack-hmm.*"

Miss Jackson then made her way to the teachers' coffee room to retrieve a misplaced cup of coffee. She returned fifteen minutes later with a large box of stickers that read "Stop Smoking" and handed them out to us kids.

As she handed out the stickers to the class, I noticed that her breath stank -- not at all like coffee -- but mysteriously a lot like cigarette smoke. This had me stumped, for I knew that my teacher did not smoke cigarettes. She must have been chewing on some cigarette-flavoured mints or a cigarette-tasting gum that I didn't see on the candy shelf at the store. I knew this because, in my young mind, my teacher was a saint and maybe even an angel.

Of course, we kids were not going to start smoking after we learned this new-found indoctrination from the saint. As for the few kids that did smoke, we would have to apply some tough love to these students until they stopped smoking. These kids were now scorned, shunned, and labelled as black sheep. Enemies of the good crowd.

They were cast into the bottomless pit of rejection with the very brightest students, the overweight kids, and kids like myself who were thought to be "stupid," and basically any kid that was not a "brat"...for "popular" meant "spoiled brat," in their minds. Of course, I was considered as one of the dumb "slow" kids because I had failed a grade in school, but I joined into this tough love approach against these black sheep, anyways. In my mind, I was hoping this would get me "in" with this envied pack of savage wolves, "The Cool Kids," and out of the bottomless pit of rejection.

This intense-pressure tactic did not quite work out so well on our fellow classmates, who were early smokers, in getting them to kick the habit as initially intended. It did, on the other hand, over the years, work quite effectively in getting those black sheep kids to stop coming to school altogether. In the ensuing years, the public school campaigns abruptly changed from, "Smoking Is Bad For You... Just Look At These Lungs!" to the new signs that then read, "Please Stay In School!" This was due to the inexplicably higher dropout rates in the public school system.

The words of our teachers, freshly planted in our ears, spurred us kids into action like a faithful band of troops. Mom did always say, "Do what the teacher tells you to," and, "Give your very best, my little angels," -- so Nedge, Calvin, and I swore to go out and rid the world of evil smokers. Our whole world, outside of school of course, consisted of our two smoking parents, Becky and Elvis, at home. Instead of getting them to quit the habit stone-cold, like we anticipated would happen overnight, our parents' habit of one pack of cigarettes a day quickly grew into three packs a day, which made them look like a smoke stack on a coal-burning electricity plant. They also developed a real nervousness, especially when they were around us boys. They started to have some trust issues.

It seemed that Mom and Dad didn't appreciate our efforts, in helping them stop smoking and quitting their addiction to the cigarettes, very much at all. If they did appreciate our efforts, they did not show it unless you count that uncontrolled eye-twitch. It sure looked like a wink of approval to us boys at the time.

We three boys thought of some very clever ways to help Mom and Dad. Yet, not all of our ideas were all that effective in getting our parents to abandon this evil habit. My brothers and I did our best though. Calvin, my youngest brother, declared, "We will be the much-needed incentive for Mom and Dad and help them kick this evil habit before they are dead, you know, like next week. This is for their own good."

Nedge and I responded to his words with great enthusiasm.

When we told Mom of our desire to help her and Dad fix this problem of theirs, Mom said they did not really need our eager help in this area of their lives, but cleaning up our filthy rooms would be a great deal of help, to start with! She spoke jokingly, of course, from her humorous side.

Shortly after being sent to our room to clean it, our great military minds gathered in our top secret location in our bedroom, which, in our minds, was well-concealed by scattered T-Shirts, pajamas, and toys, which were all strategically placed to disguise our location. This was really effective, maybe too effective, for we would almost get lost in there, to the point that we could barely find the bedroom door. But those are the drawbacks of having great military camouflage and having a young 3-Star General in the makings, leading the way.

Nedge, Calvin, and myself gathered here to discuss this coming military battle. At the moment, I only had a skeleton of a crew, which would have to do with such short notice. The military platoon was thin for lack of cousins and friends that would have filled-out the platoon, but my brothers were brave souls for the coming battle to eradicate all smokers.

Calvin's Big Plan

Calvin's plan was to go in with some, "Direct action manoeuvres and right to the point, like this sticker shows," he said as he pointed to the stickers in his hand, which had been given to him by his school teacher as well.

After our military mission briefing, the first course of action that Calvin took was direct and to the point. He just boldly, with a great deal of focus on fulfilling the military operation, walked right up to Mom, while she was happily preoccupied with watering her plants. A freshly lit cigarette was hanging out of her mouth.

Calvin ripped the cigarette from her puckered lips, swiftly thrust it to the floor, and started stomping upon it with both feet, all the while proclaiming the evils of smoking to our dear mother. This brought a great deal of shock to Mom, in having her cigarette so abruptly snatched from her mouth. Her eyes bulged out to the maximum that human eyes can bulge! With her bulging eyes, Mom's face could have easily been mistaken for the face of a spooked octopus.

Calvin's plan was sound, but it wasn't well thought-out, for the flaw in his plan was in throwing the cigarette onto the good living-room carpet. The cigarette quickly burned a dime-sized hole in the carpet, before Calvin could stomp it to death with both feet. Although his stomping jumps were very impressively high, he had trouble connecting with the cigarette underneath. Mysteriously, he completely missed the cigarette with each pounding jump.

Seeing the burning cigarette tossed to the carpet, in horror, Mom instinctively went to try to retrieve it before it burned a hole in her new carpet. As Mom's hand reached for the cigarette, Calvin's feet came down on Mom's hand, causing her hand to be stomped on with a great deal of foot-squashing power.

This made Mom's eyes bug out once again, and made her squeak with pain. Her face showed signs of agony and tears filled her wincing eyes. *"AHH, Oh, Ouch, EEEK,"* escaped out of her mouth, with each thud of Calvin's boots squashing down on her hand.

Who would have guessed that Calvin would have landed on Mom with all three stomps? One of the jumps even appeared to have landed halfway up Mom's arm. At least, that's where one of the swelling red marks was forming in the shape of the zigzag boot tread from the bottom of his boot.

With Calvin's first jump, Mom had reached for her burning smoke underneath Calvin, just as he landed upon her right hand. With this pain now coming from her hand, she instinctively pulled her right hand out of the line of danger, but then stuck out her left hand to retrieve the cigarette, before the cigarette caused more damage to the carpet. This was done just as Calvin's feet were coming down a second time. It is a known fact that, to a mom, a new carpet triumphs over broken and bleeding fingers, but I could be mistaken... the addiction to cigarettes can be a powerful thing. Perhaps Mom didn't care about the carpet at all. Now that I think about it, she could have been craving a drag of smoke. That left hand also got squished, and, for whatever reason, she reached back in with her right hand and arm, to take a second stomping on that hand. Perhaps the game -- paper, rock, scissors -- was etched in her head at that very moment, like a pair of crossed wires of instinct of her mind making unexplainable impulses through her hands.

Perhaps Private Calvin will have to be trained to not get so focused on a mission that he forgets where the stomps are landing. And at the very least, he should be trained to keep his eyes open when he is jumping so erratically. Someday, somebody just might

get injured. He could have twisted an ankle or something. His stomps were most certainly going to need to be brushed up with some military training, for I had noticed one of Calvin's boot laces had been far to loose and had come untied.

Calvin's plan had been to wear heavy boots, so he wouldn't get his feet burned by the hot cigarette when he jumped on it to put it out. This, of course, made all the sense in the world to me, the 3-Star General, because obviously Mom would not want to see Calvin get a burn injury to his foot by stomping on a burning cigarette.

When Calvin initially snatched the cigarette from her lips, he startled Mom and she spilled the whole jug of water, which she had been using to water the house plants, onto the floor. Amazingly, the water completely missed the plants and the burning cigarette, but thoroughly soaked her full pack of cigarettes and the rest of the carpet. Her pack of cigarettes must've fallen out of her plaid shirt pocket when she had gone to retrieve the burning cigarette, as the full pack of cigarettes had been flattened by Calvin's boots crushing on them.

Mom then sent Calvin to his room, which had been temporarily converted into a military prisoner stockade, for the rest of the day.

Not easily deterred from the plan of saving the lives of our parents, once Calvin was released sometime later from the stockade, he sneaked over to Mom's unguarded pack of cigarettes and broke them all into small, wee-little pieces. Although creative, this was not all that effective. So with a march to the stockade to become a permanent Prisoner-Of-War, Calvin's campaign was ended for good with running an additional twenty laps around the house.

As Mom marched him right back to the make-shift stockade in front of her, he tried reasoning, "Mom, Mom, w-a-i-t... This isn't necessary, it's for your own good. Honest. Cross my heart. Your cigarettes were just carelessly laying around, and I thought maybe you'd even lost them."

Calvin would not be moving up to Lieutenant First-Class anytime soon, because it was apparent he was moving back to boot-camp, after his extended period in the stockade was over. I do give him strong points for at least trying a retreat manoeuvre, when the plan of attack went sour.

He first suggested, "Maybe the cigarettes just fell apart on their own?"

But my mom was really smart. She knew that all those cigarettes wouldn't fall apart by themselves. She was a smart lady.

Calvin offered, just before Mom confined him in the military stockade, "Maybe they could all be taped back to together again... or maybe even some glue would work?"

I could only assume that Calvin had not read the story of Humpty Dumpty in school yet, for he was a full two years younger than me.

Nedge and I figured we would help Calvin out a little. What are bothers for? So we put the wee-little pieces of cigarette nicely back into the package for Calvin. Then we replaced the new pack of cigarettes that were on the table, with the pack of broken cigarettes so that Mom would not forget to "fix them". Perhaps the Humpty Dumpty pieces could be turned into something good, like scrambled eggs. Nedge and I then went to go play in the living-room, feeling good that we were doing some good in the world.

Moments later, we could hear Mom yell from the dining room.

"CALVIN! Now, what have you done to this pack!?!" she hollered as she opened what she thought was a new pack of cigarettes, just to find all the small, little pieces jammed in the small cardboard box, staring back at her. "I want forty laps around the house, now!"

There was little point in interrupting Mom's train of thought to explain how we had helped out around the house, and Nedge and

I both felt a strong urge to go play outside in the sandbox for a while.

Nedge's Sticker Propaganda

It was now up to the wise wits of our brother, Private Nedge. Nedge would use a more subtle, tactical approach.

Friday after school, when the school bus dropped us off at our home, we came in armed with an large arsenal of green and white stickers from school.

They read, "Smoking Is Bad For Your Lungs," and "Stop Smoking, Before It Kills You," along with other catchy lines like, "Second-Hand Smoke Kills Your Kids, DEAD!" or something like that. These stickers made a real impact and prodded urgency into the reader. All of these stickers had a big red circle, with a line crossing out some broken cigarettes, cigars, and pipes.

These were mostly all very large stickers, and the first sticker was quickly put on Nedge's yellow lunch box. His lunch box, that once had the comic book "Avengers" action scene on it, now had a "Stop Smoking!"sticker stuck on it. The sticker was so large that it wrapped all the way around to the back of his lunch box, like a poorly-wrapped Christmas present.

As we three boys ran into the house after

school, Mom said, "I'm going to go clean the bathroom. You boys, go play outside for twenty minutes."

Once back outside, Nedge drew up to me and said, "Hey, Peter, I need all of your stickers. I have some super good ideas of where to put the stickers, but my own stickers won't be enough!"

I had a few ideas of my own for my stickers. But with reluctance, I gave up all of my stickers, which were like a handful of highly guarded hand-grenades to Nedge. Sacrifices need to be made in times of tight military-ammunition sticker rations, to win a battle or two. And sacrifices would need to be made to win the war -- to save all our lives from the smokey environment around us, before death came upon us by the weekend.

Nedge, now being well-armed with my sticker rations plus his own, went to work and would do what he could to be a shining light to the eyes of the blind and misguided souls; meaning, our death-destined parents. He first started with the large car bumper, on which he placed the well-fitting, foot-long sticker containing the slogan, "Second-Hand Smoke Kills Your Kids!" We were going to be a leading example, in a very public way, that smokers were going to be dealt with severely. This dealing would be accomplished with our new-found love of the propaganda stickers.

With the rest of the stickers in hand, Nedge then went on with his mission. Like the good soldier he was, he started with the camouflage. Calvin and I helped him with his camouflage by first putting a healthy layer of warpaint on Nedge's face for battle. We were poor country kids, so we had to improvise with mud, which we had lots of, instead of using real warpaint. Calvin also suggested that Nedge use something to mask his scent, but it was quickly voted down for none of us wanted to touch any of Calvin's secret scent collection, which he had been saving for such a military manoeuvre. His collection contained: ripe cow manure scent -- rotting meat from a deceased prairie gopher that the tom cat must have killed for his lunch and then forgot about it for three days -- and some rotting turkey eggs that had being abruptly abandoned by the hen turkey around Thanksgiving time.

The rotting eggs could have easily been used as some good, safe, non-lethal hand grenades; but using the eggs as a scent killer could possibly turn Nedge's body green -- and his face would have most certainly turned green from the stench.

We figured the uncontrolled gagging noises Nedge would have been making from the scent options that were available to him, would have given his position away, for the enemy would have smelled Nedge coming from ten miles away. Perhaps if the enemy had a bad cold or if they could not smell, like the dung beetles... then maybe, but our parents had no such impairment at the time.

Within minutes of Nedge sneaking into the house through a basement window, he went to the task. Placing hundreds of stickers in the house, he started with the source of our adversity -- in our parents' bedroom.

Some stickers, he put in subtle places and some he didn't make so subtle to the eyes.

A few stickers would be staring our parents right in the face from the middle of their dresser mirror, and from their wedding photo hanging on the wall. There was at least two stickers for every bedroom wall.

The best part was that the stickers would still be stuck there for the next morning and forevermore, thanks to the superglue on the back of the stickers. These stickers would give our blind and misguided parents the subtle nudge in the right direction, that they needed to stop smoking before they perished over the weekend, like old cabbages.

Minutes later, as Nedge was fleeing our parents' bedroom, trying to slip out unnoticed, he just so happened to run right into Mom. She had a way of always suddenly appearing at the most inconvenient times.

She then backtracked Nedge's steps into her bedroom to see a large "Stop Smoking" sticker smack-dab in the middle of the mirror staring back at her, along with the array of other stickers glued onto her bedroom walls. The shock brought on by the stickers, prevented Mom from seeing this as being a nice surprise.

Mom was surprised alright, so that was a win for Nedge's efforts. But the win was short-lived, for Nedge was promptly sent back to her bedroom with a rag, a squirt-bottle containing some chemicals, and a bucket of soapy water to scrub off the stickers. The chemicals she gave him to use contained some strong fumes that had a way of burning the eyes of the user, even if you didn't accidentally get a squirt or two in your eyes when pressing the trigger on the bottle, while looking at the end of the nozzle. This cleaning task painfully took Nedge the next two hours, with his blood-shot and burning eyes, to undo the fifteen seconds of work which it took to put the stickers up!

Calvin and I would have helped him out, of course, with cleaning the stickers off, but they were sure sticky. Who could have known that those stickers had state-of-the-art glue on their backings? This glue later led to the discovery of the world's first military superglue for propaganda posters, and was also the first glue used on sticky tape to remove the hairs from women's legs and their upper-lips.

With this new-found knowledge of how difficult it was going to be to remove the stickers, Calvin and I made a change in our plans.

Calvin informed Nedge of the good news, "Hey, Nedge! Peter and I need to do some work in the sandbox, building a highway for our toy trucks and cars... so while you are busy over here on the walls, we will be busy working on that there new highway in the sandbox, okay?"

I chimed in, sharing some wisdom of our plan, "It's always a real good idea to spread out the workload, and we may even let you play on our new highway, once you're done over here. Don't worry about your cars getting in our way in the sandbox, we'll have have lots of time to build a real nice car impound for those cars until you return. Then you can get them released from the car impound... for a small fee."

As we fled the room, we could hear Nedge's voice whining behind us, "Guys, please...help me."

I shouted back over my shoulder, "If you hurry, you can get your cars out of the impound before they go to the auto-wreckers."

Some two hours later, Calvin and I returned to the house, exhausted after constructing our fine highway and car impound. After drinking a glass of orange juice to cool down after working so hard, as some of the world's finest sandbox construction workers, we then made our way back to Nedge, who was working on the removal of the last two stickers from Mom's bedroom walls.

Nedge was so glad to see us through his watery-red eyes. We pitched in to help him remove the last two stickers from the wall. Nedge appreciated our help very much, which made us feel so good, and he cracked his first smile in two hours.

He quipped, "I can't feel my arms anymore... can you see what's in my eyes? They hurt and burn. I can't seem to rub out them chemicals." Then he continued in a more gleeful tone, "But hey, guys, good thing Mom didn't see the fifty stickers I stuck up in her closet!"

He was now laughing at his own joke, and Calvin and I joined in his roar of laughter. We finished helping Nedge scrub out the last sticker from the wall, along with a layer of paint. All three of us boys then left our parents' bedroom.

We passed by Mom, who was just coming into the house at this point after running an errand outside. She said, "I need a sweater from my closet, it's getting windy outside. You boys put a coat on if you are heading outside."

"Ok, Mom," we answered in unison.

As we were getting our jackets from the bootroom closet, we heard a familiar roar coming from inside of Mom's bedroom at the opposite end of the house. This noise easily could have been the roar of a jungle lion, but nope, it was coming from our mom. "NEDGE! MY WALLS, MY PAINT, MY MIRROR! Where did... what, did... what? What? More stickers, in my closet?! AND ON MY DRESSES!!?" She stammered out her words while surveying her bedroom and the inside of her closet.

I knew this was, indeed, Mom's voice.

Nedge wailed, "Hey, you guys, where are you going? Don't you fellows want to help me?" as Calvin and I were now high-tailing it out the front door again, for at least the next three hours to play in the sandbox that suddenly needed its highways upgraded to freeway status.

Calvin chirped as we left, "Don't worry, Nedge. We'll have that auto-wreckers built, as well. If you hurry, you may have time to rip off a couple of doors from your cars, too." After this, Mom was on the lookout for big green and white stickers.

-- Hours later (once the feeling returned to

his arms), Nedge, not easily detoured, quickly came up with an alternative game plan that would be less painful on his arms and eyes. It was time for a subliminal mission. He called it's code name, "Help, Can't Breathe". This plan would take some equipment to help drive home the point that smoking was bad.

The next time our family went to town some days later, Nedge was armed with some new equipment which he tucked under his coat. We five kids, headed to the car with a great deal of childish fighting, as we fought for our lives to be the last one into our family's four-door car. The car was yellow in colour and burned gas like a modern city power plant... these were the days when Chrysler cars meant a power plant on wheels for the whole family to enjoy.

Running speed laps around the car was part of the routine of us kids getting into the car. The skirmish was just shy of biting and eye gouging, as we worked to position ourselves just right to win the car ride prize... the seat beside the door.

For we all hoped, that with the right timing, we could be the kid that was the farthest away from a car door, so that we could be the last one into the car, while simultaneously giving Mom the visual effect that we were, indeed, trying to obey her by getting into the car, as quickly as possible for the trip to town.

With a screeching crack, like a bullwhip booming upon our ears, Mom bellowed, “STOP RUNNING! OR ELSE!” as she instructed us to get into the car with her pointer finger. Our wide laps of desperation abruptly ended -- much like a game of freeze tag. Mom’s words, which were speaking volumes of devastation, were enough to send fear up and down our spines.

We were young, and we liked another day of living; so this brought our feet to an abrupt, screeching halt and we climbed into the car, with fate deciding where we would sit for the journey to town.

It was not so much the door which we fought so hard for, as it was that window in the door that was our hope of salvation. This window could be rolled down with that magical, electric, silver toggle switch that was placed on the armrest of the car door. It was this switch that was so vital to the “survival of the fittest,” in the soon-to-be toxic, tobacco smoke-filled car. That little toggle switch gave us the power of the ancient Roman dictator, Caesar -- to roll down the window or not -- at our own will.

Without a doubt, the car’s bumper had rightly received Nedge’s slogan sticker, “Second-Hand Smoke Kills Your Kids!” For within moments of shutting the car door, we would be choking on the accumulating smoke from the factory of approximately forty packs of cigarettes being smoked by our parents in a single sitting. The key was to not let Mom or Dad catch us touching the toggle switch, as we tried to escape the gagging capsule of torture in this tightly-sealed car.

If you were fortunate enough to win this prized door-seat, which was like winning the lottery, you would then be able to open the window a sliver of a crack, to escape the cigarette smoke in the car without our parents noticing.

You also would have triumphed over your siblings and could stand as kingpin, the whole trip to town with the power of the switch within your fingertips. You would be one of the few survivors that had been able to escape the force of the gagging plume of smoke that was rapidly filling the car.

Today, this cloud of toxic smoke would be most certainly beyond the lung capacity of a single soul for the survival of life on earth, but we were tough stuff back then... choking to death, yes, but tough. This is why we call it a miracle that we are still alive to this day.

If our parents did spot the backseat window open, they would yell back at us, "Do that window up, now! You're letting out all the air, and stop that ridiculous fake coughing."

Another common theme was, if they were in a kind mood, "Get that window up, and put your head back inside, before it gets torn off by on-coming traffic!"

Otherwise, if our parents were not in a so patient mood, they would just start zipping up the window using the driver's side toggle switch, with your extremities still hanging out the window. The extremities consisted of: your head, arms, fingers, nose, and, occasionally, the entire upper-half of one's body. The toggle switch on the driver's side had the ability to control all four side-windows of the car.

It was this lovely feature that the salesman at the car lot so kindly pointed out to Dad and Mom, when the deal was not going so well. After this enlightening moment, of the true power of Caesar at the flick of a switch, it was all, "We'll take it! We'll take it!" coming from our parents.

Shortly after starting out on the twenty-minute car ride to town that day, Mom was well on her way of putting one cigarette down her lungs, after another. She didn't even need to take a break in between cigarettes. She would only need to light the next cigarette with the already lit one, which was now just a smouldering stub in her hand, before it burned her fingers.

This chain-smoking event was what we kids encountered first-hand as youths. The smoking would only stop for a short window of time. A break between cigarettes at times, was needed to let the smoke fog lift inside the car long enough so that Mom could actually see the road out of the front windshield again. This was needed to not just give our bloodshot eyes a short break, but also to give our lungs a chance to catch a breath.

About halfway to town, with the car now-filled to maximum capacity with the typical cigarette smoke, Nedge calmly pulled out his concealed, secret weapon: a swimming snorkel and mask from underneath his jacket. He then put the snorkel and mask onto his head, and intelligently shoved the breathing tube out the window, which he had opened about an inch. He sucked in some fresh air, his face being safely sealed within the face mask of the scuba gear by the rubber band that was pulling from around the back of his head, to hold the mask tight to his face. To me, this was brilliant and also very funny. But Mom thought it to be something other than funny.

Mom had a unique ability of seeing things that were behind her, from out of the back of her head. With lighting-fast speed, she now jerked her head around and stared Nedge in the face.

Then she grabbed the face mask with one of her hands to remove the mask from Nedge's head, but it did not budge much for the mask was still attached to Nedge's head by the rubber band.

She did all this while juggling two cigarettes in her other hand and using her knees to guide the steering wheel, for the one new cigarette was in the process of being lit by the spent cigarette nub. This act would have been good for professional jugglers at the best of times, but my awe-inspiring Mom was doing this all while driving at high-speeds on a freshly-gravelled country road, which was like driving over a million loose marbles.

The gravelling of the road was in progress, and a gravel truck had just dropped a new load of gravel in one large pile in the middle of the road. Mom, at this point, was not aware of this, as she was a bit preoccupied. These were the days before warning signs were placed beside the road by the work crews.

The only sign given would be when one's vehicle plowed into the giant pile of gravel that had just appeared out of nowhere. The only way the country neighbours would know that the road was in the process of being gravelled was from the country gossip mill which was fed from the first guy up the road, telling of his close call of running into the pile of gravel left in the middle of the road.

Sometime later that week, the pile would then be spread out by the country grader, if it had not already been spread out by the fifty country vehicles hitting it, over the course of a week.

Farmer Garth, who dodged that first close call, picked up the phone and called his next-door neighbour, "Hey, Ted, we're finally getting some gravel on the five-mile stretch."

Ted inquired, "It's about time we got gravel. You wouldn't happen to remember exactly where the pile was dropped, would you?"

Farmer Garth replied, "Oh, somewhere between mile one and mile five, on the five-mile stretch. Ah, I was... ah... too busy looking at the crops growing to take note, but it's there."

Ted responded with, "Good to know, good to know," then he hung up the phone and called the next neighbour and so on, and the country gossip mill would spread the news.

Now, Mom always drove like a NASCAR racer at the speed-way, even when she had the added challenge of driving on gravelled roads. Often from the back seat, we kids would add sound effects like, *"Rrann, grrrr, errr... CRASH, BOOM! Aaaa,* I'm dying... oh no! The car is now on fire*! AHHHH,* help me, help me*!"* which would heighten the excitement, but our sound effects were not appreciated very much by our mother. So when the giant gravel pile suddenly appeared right in the middle of the road in front of our car, Mom was driving at her usual racing speed.

The family car tore up through one side of the pile of gravel, which had been blocking the road for the smaller cars. Our car then took flight from off the top of this large gravel pile. We soared though the air! This was a fun ride for us kids, and our stomachs sunk deep into our laps. Then a terrible, grinding noise filled our ears, and exciting sparks flew by the windows along with a spray of gravel.

The gravel tore off all-four hubcaps, all at once, and we watched them soar into the air like flying-saucers and then land in the ditch along the side of the road. This was followed by the muffler being torn-off, and then spat out the back of the car like a twisted cannonball. Now our car made a sound like a hot-rod at the Monster Car Show that had just won the crash-up derby. This spectacle would have had stuntmen seriously impressed and Hollywood knocking at our door, begging Mom to join the movie industry.

Mom let go of Nedge's scuba mask at about the point that the hubcaps left the car, in an attempt to grab the steering wheel to regain control of the car, even though at this point, it did very little good to help control the now-flying yellow submarine.

The scuba mask, that Mom had momentarily grasped in her hand, had resisted her attempts to snatch it from Nedge's head. This was due to the rubber band wrapped around the back of Nedge's head, holding the mask in place. Abruptly, Mom had released her grip on the mask when it was a good six to eight inches away from Nedge's face, to grab the steering wheel with both hands. She had decided to let it go when there was no hope of wrestling the mask into the front seat without detaching Nedge's head from his body, which is not an easy task to preform, because typically the body likes to stay attached to the head whenever possible.

Mom's yanking on the mask had pulled Nedge's unwilling head and body, momentarily, over into the front seat before being smacked backwards, as she released the mask. Nedge fell back into the backseat, the mask whacking him in the face. The mask returned and settled back into its place over Nedge's now protruding eyes, just as quickly as it had left.

Mom made the decision that driving was now a major priority, as she grabbed the steering wheel with both hands.

We kids all yelled in harmony with a long, "*WHEEE...*," and Mom yelled, "*AAAAAAAW*!"

Then we all held our breaths as we could now feel our stomachs making their way up into our throats, after being so far down into our toes just a moment earlier.

The car's landing came some minutes later, as a new wave of fresh gravel now soared over the hood of the car like a roaring swath, removing any remaining paint still on the car. Mom wrestled to bring the car into control and to a stop.

A moment later, I looked around to see if we were all still alive after this incredible descent from the heavens. We sat there in silence, but only for a fading moment as the action was not yet over. I saw, with my shocked eyes, that Nedge was now fighting a small fire in his hair, with his now-flailing hands.

In his hair, that's where Mom's smoke ended up, I realized with a chuckle.

The fire had started from one of Mom's cigarettes. Nedge's hands went *smack, smack,* to the top of his burning head of hair, then there was a pause. Then *SMACK, SMACK* a little harder for the second go-around, but that smouldering cigarette just would not die, being lodged in his thick hair, no matter how hard Nedge smacked around on the top of his head.

This is where Calvin and I joined in, to help with the smacking at his head. We had no, real set order to the smacking, but Calvin and I did try to whack at the fire real hard to get it out.

I was about to belt out a roaring laugh, joining in with my other siblings who were laughing and whacking at Nedge, when my laughter abruptly turned to horror. I began feeling some very unwanted excitement now erupting from my own seat, between my thighs, known as the crotch area. I had, of course, found the partner cigarette nub to Mom's other smoke. This caused me to smack and leap about in a less-than-joyful fashion, to escape this mayhem brewing on the car seat under my backside. As I smacked at my crotch area, trying to put out the fire, I could see my other siblings looking at me with a great deal of excitement. There was even eagerness in their eyes to whack at the curl of smoke between my legs. This would not be very welcome help at all, in my eyes, to have the seat of my pants smacked upon by my sibling's flailing arms and hands!

Mom finally brought the car to a stop at the side of the road. We replanted our stomachs in their rightful places and doused the small fires with a half-drank bottle of stale cola that Calvin had found rolling on the floor of the car. We returned Mom's cigarettes, which had flew from her hand without warning when we hit the gravel mound. Mom got out of the car to look at the damage and to make sure that all-four wheels were still attached to the car. In a bit, we were back driving again, but far slower than before, with Mom now scolding us for all our unwanted antics. These types of performances did make for some pretty good entertainment in the backseat, even if it meant not being able to sit down for a week.

After our car's test flight, I thought it was a good idea to cut Mom some slack, in our quest to kill her smoking habit. Her nerves seemed to be a bit on the frazzled side, and the intensity of her smoking had also picked up steam, by a notch or two.

A bit of time would not hurt in the healing process of my small, affected burn area, either. Nedge, on the other hand, only lost a good chunk of his hair from the top of his head.

Peter Adds Toothpicks

A few weeks later, when most of the smoke had cleared, I figured that it was my turn to share my loving side to the smokers' world.

I'm so kindhearted and thoughtful, I mused to myself, as I painstakingly inserted a toothpick in each one of Mom's cigarettes. I even managed to put in a few nice firecrackers, for good measure. I reasoned that Mom would think it was the cigarette company making the defective cigarettes, because defects happen, sooner or later. I would have showed Dad the same loving-affection, but for some odd reason, he never let his cigarettes out of his sight, like Mom did.

I waited patiently for Mom to light a cigarette, to see what would happen. But she was just taking forever.

What's happened to her chain smoking...? Perhaps we're making a difference and are whittling her down too much?

I really was getting impatient. I decided that I would need to take Mom's cigarettes over to her, where she was busy cleaning the house.

Out loud I sweetly asked, "Mom, don't you need a smoke, yet? You're taking forever. Here, take one."

She retorted, "Why... what did you do to them?" as she pulled a cigarette from the pack and stared suspiciously at its one end, like some criminal investigator. She was acting as if she thought something was up.

Good thing I took all that extra time and

care, embedding the toothpicks just right the first time, like a skilled, honest criminal, so that Mom couldn't see them with her naked eye. I silently praised myself for my good handiwork with a great deal of self satisfaction.

Then the moment, that I had long and gleefully anticipated, came. Mom started to light the smoke. She sucked-in with a hard inhale to get it lit. Black billows of smoke poured out from the cigarette.

Wow, I thought. *It must be the cigarette that I put the three toothpicks in, to triple the effect. It's only disappointing that it isn't the one with the firecracker in it.*

Mom was now coughing and gagging for air, "*KAA... WOOFF... KAAA... WOF... HHA*!" She had the appearance of a backfiring car, as large barks of black smoke began pluming out of her mouth. This was followed by great wheezes on the inhale, and her eyes were really starting to water, but at least she had quit puffing on the cigarette temporarily.

She coughed and choked out, "What did you do to it—*KAAA... WO... FFHH*?" gasping for air, as her burning eyes rolled around in her head. She was fleeing the area like one who flees a burning building filled with deadly smoke. Black smoke was now puffing out of her nose and mouth, like a choo-choo train.

"I —*KAAF*— I know it was you! Now, tell me what you did to it!" she demanded, between the wheezes and coughs.

I could hardly come up with the nice, good fish-story that I had preplanned to tell her. I was now stammering for my words, from the shock of the effectiveness of the toothpicks. "It's... its... smoker's cough, Mom!" was all I managed to say.

She swore that it was not a smoker's cough, as I had so kindly suggested, but that it was, in fact, due to smoke tampering. She marched me to my bedroom to spend some time by myself in the stockade, wheezing as she went. But at least, I wasn't going to have to run laps.

Not all was lost, though, as I had learned three powerful lessons out of this misunderstanding.

The first lesson was that, indeed, there was a right time to give a fake humble opinion.

The second lesson: I had better work harder on my pretend pleading and begging with extra howling and baaing as to reduce the amount of time sentenced to the stockade prison, for I was getting really bored in there.

The third lesson was, I figured, I'd better get the rest of the toothpicks and the firecrackers out of Mom's cigarettes before she smoked another one.

It did make me a little grateful, that Mom got the less-potent, toothpick cigarette. One can handle only so many hours at a time in the bedroom stockade prison all alone. The firecracker just might have cured her forever from the addiction that was sucking out her soul, but I will never know.

Once I was finally let out of the stockade, which felt like months later, I looked around... *What do I see over there? Dad's left his cigarettes unguarded on the coffee table! No point, in letting the opportunity slip by, to see what really happens when a firecracker is lit on the inside of a cigarette!*

Chapter Eight

****

Work Boots

My sister Daisy was six years old, I was five; and we were buddies. Best friends. My two younger brothers were too young to be very important in our lives, especially when their wet diapers hung, swinging back and forth between their legs like wild wrecking-balls as they walked.

It was at this time in our lives, my dad Elvis

decided to build a money-making, hog-barn venture. This venture made Dad sweat bullets for the next ten years, as he struggled to pay off the bankers for his privilege of working with the most impossibly stubborn animals on the planet. However, these hogs did not just drop out the gold bricks, as my dad had so eagerly anticipated. This hog barn would house over a hundred sows which would need four separate, underground pits to contain the hogs' counterfeit "gold bricks". These concrete-lined manure pits were eight feet deep, had a spanning distance of six feet wide, and ran two hundred feet in length, resembling a long Dutch canal. This would store all of the pigs' fool's gold, which had completely lost its glorious lustre.

Now the pits smelled quite good, when they were brand-new and fresh. They just smelled like sweet concrete and tar, but once the manure dropped down into the pits from the happy pigs above, the joyful smell that once filled my nose quickly faded into the stench of toxic hog manure. The smell tar and spruce wood from the new construction, I can still smell in my nose today. It would be nice to have a flower in my garden that smelled this way, but ladies never grow flowers to please their man.

Shortly after these pits were constructed, Daisy and I came up with the marvellous idea of riding our banana-seat bikes across these empty, concrete pits whenever the construction crew took their lunch break inside my parents' house or when they went home in the evening.

Daisy and I first collected a ten-foot long, 2x6 board that we found laying around the construction site of the barn. We then put this 2x6 board over the top, across the open pit. This was not an easy task to accomplish at our age, but we were persistent and got the job done. The board then spanned the full-six feet across, to the other side of the concrete canyon. When completed, it looked like a nifty bridge.

The thrilling part was that the long canyon dropped eight feet straight down onto a concrete floor below. Unfortunately, the canyon-pit was not filled with water, but you can't win them all.

"Oh my," Daisy observed, "if we fall off the board, we might get hurt when we hit the bottom."

I replied reassuringly, "But, Daisy, at least there's no sharp rocks at the bottom."

We thought that maybe we should try to soften the fall, so we poured two ice-cream buckets of water into the canyon... even though a fall in our eyes was highly improbable, if not downright impossible. But the water we dumped in, did not even so

much as make a puddle. The water seemed to dry up as quickly as Daisy and I could pour it down into the hole on this hot June day, and so we gave up on making our canyon river.

Using our hands, we then grabbed some dirt and gravel to make a tiny dirt ramp on each end of the 2x6 board to aid our bikes in getting up, onto the board. This dirt was needed to hold the board in place, as we bounced across it on our bikes. As long as we got our speed up, we could bolt across that 2x6 board with ease. If we did not get up enough speed, Daisy and I assumed that we might get a scratch or two when we hit the bottom of the pit; and then if our bikes happened to fall on top of us, we might get a scratch or two more. So, we figured that getting up enough speed was key to the success of making it across our canyon bridge.

Now this was most certainly pleasing to us, in dodging death with our bikes, as we raced over the canyon bridge three or four times a day. This needed to be done far away from the eyes of the work crew, though, for they did not like us playing with their tools and supplies. The prime time for us to defy death was at lunch break, when the crew would be eating their lunch in our parents' house.

All of our fun came to a very unpleasant end one day, when the work crew came out of the house just as we were racing, crossing the board over the pit, on our bikes.

I had just triumphantly announced, “Hey, Daisy, look at me! No hands!”

The workers, coming out of the house, saw us crossing the bridge. With horror written all over their faces, they started running towards us, like there was a fire or something in our direction. We looked around and behind us, but Daisy and I couldn't see what all the excitement was all about.

The mean crew foreman, Mr. Steel, ran up to us and began harshly scolding us for crossing the pits with our bikes. He had a deep voice that cracked like a whip, and like his name rightly suggested, his voice slammed down on us hard, like a sledge hammer hitting a steel bar. His voice vibrated through our ears and into the uttermost parts of our souls, making us quake.

Mr. Steel thundered, “You little brats trying to bust your heads open?!? Blah, blah, blah, do you hear me, kids? blah, blah, blah...”

Then he abruptly snatched our 2x6 board-bridge away, which had taken us so long to construct over the open pit, and cast it aside with a great deal of irritation.

Mr. Steel also had two mean workers, who seemed to follow him around the worksite like a couple of gang members. They were taking orders from Mr. Steel... or more appropriately put – they were like a couple of slaves under a task-master, for you would hear, "Yes, Sir!" "Right away, Mr. Steel!" coming from the slaves that would be running wildly to obey the commands of their master. Daisy and I suspected that this wild running by the two workers to instantly perform the task was because of fear of getting a tongue whipping -- or they were just really good suck-ups.

One of Mr. Steel's sidekicks, whom we knew as Plumber Dale, was still chewing on a sandwich from lunch. In his high, squeaky voice, with numerous crumbs flying out of his mouth, Plumber Dale added, "Take away their bikes too, Mr. Steel, *(gulp)*."

And he swallowed another bite of his sandwich. Daisy shot him a wicked glare as she folded her arms across her chest to show her displeasure, but it made little difference.

The other thug we knew as Carpenter Leo. He was always grumpy, like he never got enough sleep. He was a sloppy carpenter, and he dropped nails by the hundreds. Daisy and I figured between us, that his mommy must have taken away his favourite teddy bear to make him so grumpy.

Carpenter Leo snarled, "Mr. Steel, make them clean up all the mess on the worksite as punishment, and my nails, too."

This scheme was very unpleasing to us, and I added a scowl to the mix, as the worksite was a complete mess and Carpenter Leo was the messiest of all the crew. Carpenter Leo, grumbling and complaining, would cut a board to the length he needed for the barn with the electric skill-saw. Then the leftover piece, which was normally about a foot long, would just be left right where it fell, and there were hundreds of these such pieces scattered around on the worksite. This guy was a complete slob; the worksite looked almost as messy as my bedroom. This didn't seem like a nice idea to Daisy or myself, for it would take us all day to clean up the worksite, and it was such a hot day!

"They're downright bullies to do such a crime against us little kids in taking away all of our fun for the day," I muttered to Daisy, as we went about picking up the little board-ends and putting them into a pile.

This evil act against us would stunt the careers of some very fine, circus, tightrope performers, who rode their bikes over a canyon, without using their hands on the handlebars. This performance also was done without a safety-net underneath us, so that we could woo the crowd, which was filled with thumb-sucking youngsters, wearing saggy diapers.

That's the nature of some adults. They're

just all-around, mean people, I thought to myself. *This kind of meanness deserves some revenge.*

I would realize, later in life, that revenge is something to be avoided, so that you don't wake up one morning with the air let out of all-four car tires by someone from a past generation seeking revenge. But at the time, revenge was fair game on bullies and on all-around mean people. Daisy and I would have to come up with a crafty plan that would be simple and direct in showing our displeasure of the work-crew's wicked ways.

The next day at lunchtime, Daisy and I were sitting at the dining-room table, peacefully enjoying our sandwiches and drinking some Kool-Aid, when the work crew came in for their lunch.

Carpenter Leo growled at Daisy and I, "So, you little runts finding some trouble to root your noses into today?...ha, ha." Leo chuckled as he scratched the back of his hand, and then his neck. "I've got a real treat for you kids to clean up today. Ha...ha." He was scratching himself, for he had been working with itchy fibreglass insulation that day, and had left plenty of cut scraps laying around the construction site.

His henchman friend Plumber Dale quipped in his high, squeaky voice, "That's right, Leo, they're good for nothing more than rooting in the mud. Ha, Ha. Now get out of that chair, you little pip-squeak. I'm sitting there."

I looked up at my mom as she instructed, "Up you go, Peter. Why don't you and Daisy go outside and let this nice gentleman have your chair so that he can have his lunch?"

I protested, "But, Mom, I'm not finished my Kool-Aid yet."

"Well, just drink it quick, and out you go," she kindly answered.

Now, when the work crew went in the house for their normal lunch break, it was a common practice for them to leave their work boots outside on our porch to avoid tramping dirt, tar, and whatever else might be stuck on the bottom of their boots onto my mom's clean floors. This was customary, for even the most wicked gentlemen would take their boots off outside.

As we left the house door to go outside and play, the work crews' boots laying on the porch caught Daisy's eye. She excitedly exclaimed in her soft voice, just over a whisper, "Hey, Peter, their boots! Maybe we can tie some knots in their laces?"

I agreed enthusiastically, "Good idea, Daisy!"

Our plan went flawlessly, as we tied dozens of knots into the work-crew's bootlaces. When we were done, it looked like a nice pot of spaghetti had been dumped on each boot,

but Daisy and I were not through, yet.

Daisy had another suggestion, "Maybe we could put some rocks and sand in them... even some nails would get their attention. They're too busy with pointless things, like eating and talking with Dad and Mom about the barn-project."

Through the screen door, we could overhear the work crew ratting on us, informing our parents of our fun biking adventure over the pits. They were now talking of even taking our bikes away from us, permanently! This, indeed, deserved some revenge as well.

As my two glasses of Kool-Aid now made their final rounds of nutrition through my body into my bladder, a brilliant idea came to me. *Why couldn't we give them this secondary Kool-Aid, right inside their boots for their evil ways?*

So with a shoulder-shrug of approval from Daisy, I went forward with my plan. I was able to fill both of Mr. Steel's two work boots, as I emptied my inner-tank. It is truly amazing how much liquid can be packed into one's inner-tank when the tap is closed. As for Daisy, she obviously had not been as thirsty as I had been at lunchtime.

Thankfully, Daisy was a fast thinker. (This, I believe, was because she could actually read the name on the work boots, as she had earlier informed me, “The name of the boots are ‘Work Boots’.” It’s truly hard to argue with such smart people. I thought they were just plain boots, and I stood corrected.)

So now, Daisy came up with a substitute plan for her lack of fluids in her inner-tank. She retrieved a glass of water from the facet and poured the water into one of the boots. This was far-less as impressive, but it would have to do under the tight time-restraints, before the work crew finished eating their lunch. The foreman and his two gang members would get a full-dose of revenge for their meanness.

A little later the men came out of the house still chatting away to each other. Then their chatter abruptly stopped in mid-sentence, as their eyes gazed at their knotted bootlaces in bewilderment. Then they began to laugh.

“Those little brats, they’re getting extra duty now.” Plumber Dale squeaked, and then he went about untangling the knots that were in his boot laces.

“Little practical jokers, I see,” chuckled Mr. Steel. “Too bad, you kids, don’t have laces on your rubber boots.”

Carpenter Leo growled, “Maybe, we’ll keep your bikes for good, for this little stunt,” as he shot us a scowl, with his lips puckered as he struggled to untie the knots.

Unaware of the little surprise waiting for

them, in the most unsuspecting manner, the men began to neatly push their feet into their boots. Daisy and I watched from a safe distance.

Mr. Steel quickly found the "yellow creek" and some nice sharp rocks, and a mighty grimace flashed over his face. There was a pause that hung in the air, which had the look of someone that was saying to themselves, *"This feels different, even unpleasant."* He then gave a sharp high squeak of anguish, as his toes hit the large gravel that was tucked nicely into the toes of his boots. There is nothing quite like pulling on a tight boot to find that the toe of the boot is missing and has been replaced with sharp rocks and a puddle of yellow water!

Plumber Dale was smart and caught onto the little game. He decided to dump his own boots out first, before putting his feet into a torture device, as he was now, with a wince, observing the painful, uplifted toenail of Mr. Steel. Plumber Dale tried to dump the anticipated water out of his boots, but nothing came pouring out. So figuring that Mr. Steel was just an all-around evil guy, anyways, Plumber Dale put his foot into his own boot with a laugh, relieved that he was not a target. His laughter quickly turned sour as he discovered that the tip of his boot was filled-in -- solid like a rock -- instantly turning his size-13 boot down to a much smaller size-9 boot. You never saw someone's eyebrows jerk to the top of their forehead so quickly. Apparently, the "grey dirt" that Daisy and I had found in a couple of their construction bags, when mixed with water, holds together quite nicely... like concrete.

Now, the words that came out of Plumber Dale's mouth were more than a squeal. In agony, he cried out, "*AHHH*, blah blah blah.... I will get you, little brats.... *A-H-H-H*... blah blah blah," as tears filled the bully's eyes. It appeared to Daisy and I, that he was not near as tough as Mr. Steel.

When Plumber Dale's toes went into the boots, they looked all normal; but when they came out, they were a different story. All of his toes had been bent completely backwards and looked like a bowl-full of broken pretzels. As he pulled his sock from his foot, Plumber Dale rolled unto his back, clenching his swelling, mangled toes. He had really long toes that now looked like tiny broken accordions. His pinky toe even appeared to be turned inside-out.

By this point, Carpenter Leo was pouring out a handful of shingle nails from one of his boots. As he dumped out the couple dozen nails, he even put his hand into the toe of his boot to make sure there was no concrete in there.

He smirked, "So you brats thought that you could outsmart me?"

When he was confident that there were no stray nails left inside -- after giving his boot a thorough shaking -- Carpenter Leo gingerly pulled on his first boot, expecting the worst. With no ill-effects at all, he heaved a sigh of great relief.

This built up his confidence, that his thorough boot check had been efficient enough, and he slipped on his second tight-fitting boot. There was a *pop* sound as his foot hit the sole of his boot.

Daisy and I watched as his eyebrows came clear-off the top of his head and dangled there for several moments. His mouth dropped open with a scream that one would only likely hear coming from inside the underworld.

Carpenter Leo had now found the lone nail that we had managed to pound into the heel of his boot; its point stuck straight upwards, yet was concealed by the inside boot sole. His thorough check was not quite as thorough as he had thought. Hammering one nail through the thick rubber sole had been no small task, for those soles were hard for a little kid to pound a nail into, but we figured that getting one nail into the boot was better than nothing.

With this, Daisy and I were already on the

run for our lives. Carpenter Leo's eyes, for some strange reason, were glowing red, like a beast from the underworld, and he started chasing us. But Daisy and I got away, and hid in a pile of building materials from the barn, which hadn't been put up yet.

The workmen left that evening, all wincing and wearing painful grimaces on their faces. The pairs of boots my dad had supplied to replace Mr. Steel's wet boots and Plumber Dale's ruined, concrete-filled boots, were too small for their large feet. Apparently, Dad only had size-10 substitute footwear for them to use. All three workmen went hobbling about on painful feet for days, because of their wicked ways that had been pointed at nice little kids.

Chapter Nine

⁂⁂*

Call Of The Lighter

I was listening to the radio, while I was enjoying drinking my morning cup of coffee at the kitchen table. They were announcing that the Forestry was issuing a fire ban, and were enforcing this ban with heavy fines.

The Forestry is really flexing their muscles this year, they are getting serious, I mused to myself.

This was not the kind of news I needed to hear, as I had been planning for a couple of days to burn those evil, dead Canadian thistles that were in my front yard. This spot, in the yard, had finally dried out after two years of being too soaking wet to mow. Now that it was spring and the grass had finally dried out, I figured I would just skip the work of mowing altogether, and just burn the dead thistles instead. This was a problem, for Forestry was not allowing any open fires!

How rude of them! They didn't even give me a chance to show how careful a McVanBuck could be with fire, for the McVanBucks have a mountain of experience with wild fires. That had to add up to something, didn't it?

A few minutes later, my neighbour Mr. Brown came driving into our yard in his beat-up, rusty car, looking for a visit and coffee.

My wife Joy quickly threw open a window, saying to me, “I sure hope Mr. Brown took a bath this time before coming over. You know, it took a week for my plants to recover from their wilt the last time he came over.”

As Mr. Brown knocked on our front door, the smell from outside came wafting in through the open window, hitting my nose, making my knees wobble.

Joy, hesitating, sucked in some air and began to hold her breath before letting the rank old farmer and his fog of death into the house. The door was hardly open, before Mr. Brown’s foot appeared in the crack of the door, just in case Joy was going to change her mind about letting him in.

As he took a seat at our table and I poured him some coffee, I said, “You’ve been skinning some skunks again, I see.” And I thought to myself, *It must have been a ripe rotten skunk; the stink’s so rank that it could peal the paint off the walls and a layer of flesh off of my eyeballs.*

He replied, “No, just that dandy-sized skunk last month. Why do you ask? ...Hey, did you hear about the fire ban they just issued?”

“Just heard this morning, but I don’t think that applies to people that are real careful,” I responded. I’m thinking nobody’s gonna notice if I burn that little patch of weeds out front there.”

“Man, you’ve got to be a near-fool to burn. Forestry’s sure to catch you. Why... they even caught me once... and I was sure they weren’t looking,” insisted Mr. Brown.

The fine must have sucked every dime out of him to the point that he couldn’t pay for his own food, as I suddenly noticed Mr. Brown slipping his coffee spoon into my bowl of breakfast oatmeal.

Once Mr. Brown had finished off my bowl of oatmeal and his cup of coffee, he was up and out the door announcing, “Well, you’re an idiot, McVanBuck, to burn. But I must be on my way; heard Mrs. Fletcher was doing her baking today. She might need a hand gettin' it out of the oven."

As the door closed behind him, I began to tell Joy that apparently, according to Mr. Brown, the McVanBucks are crazy, fire weirdos... I guess my kin are the only weirdos these days who don't listen to pointless fire bans, and such is the plot of life.

Mr. Brown's ghost remained clinging to the inside of our house for some hours after. But he had made me second-guess myself, maybe the fumes from his body were getting to my brain. So I decided to make a quick phone call to get some counsel from the best source that I knew... my dad, Elvis McVanBuck, the greatest fire legend to ever walk the Canadian prairies. Dad was wise to the ways of fire, so I inquired of him if I should burn or not, even with a potential fine.

His wise counsel was, "When a burnin' needs burnin', ya burn it! When pig crap needs shovelin', ya shovel it. And as for that fine, they can only fine you, if you get caught."

This sounded pretty wise and solid to me.

When I related to Joy this wise counsel that Dad had given me, she said, "Well, just don't start any fires out there today. Please open that other window over there, honey. My eyes are still burning." Grabbing the fly swatter, she whacked at a couple of stray fleas who had obviously fled from Mr. Brown to what they had thought was a safer area.

"Don't be silly," came my reply. "Do you really think I would be an idiot and start a fire on this fine, beautifully sunny, hot, crispy-dry day with a fire ban on? Besides, my dad says that the Forestry doesn't really fine smart people, anyways."

Joy countered, "Well, your dad Elvis can be overly aggressive when it comes to fire. I've heard all those fire stories from your kin, and there's something wrong with your dad's counsel."

While she was still speaking, I saw a lighter laying on the kitchen counter. The lighter was tempting me, like a secret voice of my past, calling me, "Peter... Peter... listen to Elvis. Don't you love a little fire? We are not talking about a large fire, we are talking a little baby-size Elvis fire. *Who-o-o-o, who-o-o-o.*"

Now, I was arguing against the call of the lighter, *But what about what Joy says about Dad's counsel? You know his counsel isn't very good and often turns out very bad. I think you are*
an evil lighter.

And the lighter responded, "But your dad is wiser, and has a higher-paying, farming

I
CALL
FIR

business than you. And remember, he doesn't like you being a sissy, humour writer. A nice fire would win over his heart."

Who can argue with the voice of reason? And the lighter entered my pocket.

As I left the house, Joy repeated to me again, "Now, no fires without telling me first."

"You bet," came my very serious reply, as I patted the pocket with the lighter nestled comfortably in the bottom of it.

"Ya,Ya," I could hear Joy reply uneasily.

What a joker she can be, I thought to myself, as the house door swung shut behind me and trapped the plume of stench inside the house.

I paused on the porch to gaze upon my beautiful acreage spread, as I took a long, enjoyable arm-stretch, filling my lungs with the much appreciated fresh air. *What is this nastiness I see?* My eyes locked onto the thistle patch that blinked like a beacon at me. *Thistles! This is unacceptable!* The terrible eyesore had caught my eye, once again.

I spoke out loud to myself, "This weed patch is absolutely deplorable!"

Due to the "communistic" fire ban, I had been trying to make a mental note to ignore the long brown grass and dead Canadian thistles. These thistles, that had now polluted my front yard, were itching at me like a bad case of bedbugs. The stupid fire ban only heightened my itch to uncontrollable levels. There's nothing worse than an eyesore to turn your morning smile into an annoyed frown.

It wasn't my fault the yard looked this way. We had given up on mowing this swampy, weed-infested spot altogether, when Joy had gotten tired of pulling me and our ride-on lawnmower out of the mud with our truck.

It would be at these moments when Joy was pulling me out of the mud with our truck, that the neighbouring farmers would crawl by in their pickup trucks, on the road. These pickup-driving farmers would be taking a long look at their freshly rain-soaked wheat crops, which had received a new lake of unwanted rain overnight, creating new larger lakes.

From the lakes, the crops would be crying out, "Help.... help, you rich farmers, do something! We are drowning. Throw us a life jacket, at least!" These grain crops were struggling for their very lives, just as much as Joy was struggling with me on the ride-on lawnmower, pushing through a wave of water.

Our antics gave the farmers plenty of opportunity to gab about us, saying some mysterious words to each other while shaking their heads as their pickup trucks crawled by our yard. They believed us to be some nutty city slickers; who, two years previously, had just moved into the countryside and were trying to use our lawnmower as a boat.

This brought a great deal of embarrassment to Joy, as this only seemed to reinforce our neighbours' fears that we were nuts, and needed to be shunned out of the country, right back into the city.

Still mulling the sad state of the lawn over in my mind, I went ahead with the chores of milking the cow and feeding the chicks and turkeys. I then did the watering and weeding in the garden that needed to be done for the day.

I flew through the chores with great promptness and with such ease. With the morning chores behind me, I had time before lunch to deal with all those dead thistles in the front yard. I thought to myself once again of what an eyesore it was.

I reached in my pocket to pull out the lighter, as it was still itching at me with its relentless, nagging voice... "Get me out of here! I promise I'll behave myself this time.... I promise. You need me, more than I need you! Just look at those ugly, disgusting Canadian thistles! *Whoo...whoo!* I don't belong in this pocket, particularly when there's all those long, dead Canadian thistles to burn. *Whooo!!* Remember how intelligent writers are with fire? *Whooooo!!!*"

With a quick glance at the house window, to see if Joy was peaking out or not, I freed the little voice from my pocket. The lighter cheered for joy to be free at last. I crouched over in the thistles, the lighter in hand, to test for dryness. Yep, it was very dry and prickly.

"Ouch! You thorny little Canadian icon," I blurted out as a thistle stuck into my finger.

With that, I knew that patch was going to burn, and burn quickly once it was lit. I licked my finger and held it up in the air, to see if there was any wind. A wind can blow a fire off-course at great speeds. There were some memories of past fires that came flooding into my mind, and were now working their way into what the educated person would call "knowledge". With this "knowledge" added to the long list of other McVanBuck "knowledges," built up over the fiery years of my past, I figured I had better put some of this knowledge to use.

I needed a good, fool-proof plan, so with the McVanBuck's wise counsel in the works, I then began to formulate one in my head:

Step 1: Grass needs burning. Check!

Step 2: Test wind conditions; mild... hardly a breeze. Check!

Step 3: Need some sort of barrier between

the grass that I want to burn, and the grass next to the woods that I don't want to burn; or I'll get caught and get a fine. The lawn mower will have to do in making a barrier between the woods and thistles. Check!

Step 4: Shovel and pick nearby. Check and Check!

Step 5: Fill the water tank on the back of the truck... in case of an exceedingly-rare emergency. Check!

Within minutes, I had mowed a three-foot wide path along the edge of the woods. I took another long look at the house, and gave a long wave and smiled at Joy, who was again mysteriously peeking through the window blinds at me. One would think that she had the kids' diapers to change or something else to do; but I guess a guy can't help being so truly handsome, being hard at real work and not just the usual writing. It was just that shaking finger of hers, scolding me, that made it feel like she didn't appreciate a man doing real work. You would've thought that she was thinking that I was about to do something stupid. She should have been aware of what I was doing; it was logical -- making a very nice fire barrier.

After several passes with the lawn mower, all was set. The fire, once started, would be safely contained in the tall dead thistles, within this some fifty-by-fifty-foot quarantine zone. With that, I could hear the little voice of the lighter calling me again. Like a horse gnawing on his bit, the lighter was itching to get to work. So with the "all clear" from Joy, now that she was no longer standing at the window shaking her finger, I once again knelt down in the grass, nervously clinging to the lighter with my sweaty hands. I lit the lighter. *Poof,* there was fire.

It was at that very moment, when the fire hadn't spread even a foot in diameter, that a dirt devil came out of the heavens, slamming into my innocent little fire. The forces of the wind almost blew me off of my feet. This twisting, evil freak of the sky was making my plan go all wrong, as it sent the flames swirling into the sky above me.

The dirt devil was using the dreaded Canadian thistles as fuel for a flamethrower, shooting the thistles' fluffy, now-burning seeds up into my face, like hot ashes.

The thorns of the thistles are painful, at the best of times; they stick into your skin and then break off. This is quite annoying and painful to experience, but when they are on fire... well, it's quite the thrilling experience.

I quickly began beating the burning thistles to put out the flames; but at the same time, I was driving the thistles in further -- under my skin -- like railroad spikes being pounded into the palms of my hands.

I believe the words that came out of my mouth at that moment were simple, but to the point, *"AAAHHH...* what have I done?!"

Instinctively, my fingers clamped tightly to the top of my head, clutching my hair, as a familiar enemy from the past emerged in front of my eyes, out of nowhere.

Even with this large freak, dirt devil on the loose, I was well-prepared for such events. I'd even anticipated such a phenomenon. So all was still well ...until the dirt devil grabbed full-control of the flames, as it was now picking up all the loose, dead thistles that I had just mowed and was now tossing them into the air. It was a flaming tornado of dread. With great ease and evil on its mind, the dirt devil crossed not only the swamp, but also my well-prepared, three-foot wide barrier at the wood's edge. *Wwhoorrrshrr!* Its roaring filling my ears, as it raced into the woods, which was full of yet more dry dead leaves, sticks, brambles, and weeds.

It was at that moment, as the flames burst into the woods as an intense inferno, that I looked down at the little lighter in my hand. Somehow, it seemed that the friendly little voice was now an evil that had been just released from the underworld, like a genie from a bottle. I now know for certain, that all genies living in lighters, do give you your wish... but with a bonus dirt devil.

How could such a small little container, that was in my pocket no less than thirty seconds prior, have created such wickedness? I wondered, as the fire roared into the woods and was now consuming whole trees.

I grabbed my shovel and started wildly beating at the grass, because... well again, I was well-prepared.

I kept looking towards the house, waiting for my sweet Joy to come out and help me, but the help never came. Joy must have been changing three or four of our kids diapers all at once! It is at these moments, that mere seconds feel like long weeks. This was absolutely dreadful and unbearable, but I didn't dare leave the flaming tornado, that had now leapt into the trees, alone for a second. If I left to go and get help, then it would feel in principle, like things were out-of-control, and not just a flaming tornado burning everything down to the ground.

But I could not delay a moment longer, I was going to need the big guns. I was going to need the truck of water; perhaps I should have parked it a little closer than half-a-mile away.

So I bolted to the house, whipped the door open, and sputtered out some sort of gibberish words. But with my smouldering clothes half-falling off of my body, Joy knew what was going on right away.

She only uttered three words, "N-o-o, you didn't!"

As I followed her out the front door, I finally regained my speech, and the single word that came out of my mouth was, "Ta-da!" There was no time to hang my head in shame.

As Joy and I stood there for mere fractions of a second, it was one of those moments in which you ask yourself, "How did I become what I am?"

At least the house hasn't burned down yet, so things are still in the positive, I encouraged myself. I flung my head back and used my running legs to maximum capacity to race in the direction of my truck which had the five hundred gallons of water sitting on the back of it. This would now be my lifeline and last-saving grace to put out the inferno, before all was lost in ashes.

Once in the truck, I hurriedly drove in the direction of the fire, to try to cut it off before it spread any farther in its wild rampage. I steered the truck into the shallow ravine in the front yard, where all the dead thistles had been. The wind was carrying the fire in the opposite direction – up the hill, on the far side of this low spot. As the truck tore through the low spot, I thought to myself, *Okay, we are going to beat the fire genie.*

And just at that moment, the truck came to a sagging stop, stuck a foot-deep in the mud-drenched ground. I hadn't been aware that the ground in this low spot was still wet; really wet.

Now, this was some knowledge that could've been very helpful to know, before I drove a heavy truck onto it. Ground, it seems, can be still wet under the surface, and yet the weeds above and the surface ground be as dry as ever. This was a well-laid, entrapping illusion for a truck. *This is why we need people to learn this stuff, like myself, to help our fellow mankind before they do something foolish,* I thought. *I am seriously underestimating the power of this fire genie; it tricked me into going that way with the truck!* Fire genies are dangerous creatures! These creatures are even able to out think an experienced fire-genius McVanBuck, in ways that can't easily be explained.

The mud sunk right up to the belly of the truck, as it was obvious now, that all the water in the tank sitting on the back of the truck hadn't helped the truck get through this mud.

It was this moment that made me reflect on my life and made me go *"AAHHH."* Once again, my fingers combed through my hair, in a nervous, twitching motion, but there was a

great deal of speed in my fingers this time. Nervousness was growing exponentially inside of me like a virus.

Even though things were looking bleak and getting a bit more problematic, there was still no need for level-two fear. Fear needs to be broken down into levels, to truly be appreciated for its finer qualities. Otherwise, a McVanBuck would just look insane, from the eyes of an onlooker, right from the get-go. The onlooker may be thinking the fire was completely out-of-control at this point, and not safely contained in the recesses of the McVanBuck mind, but I still had one last safety backup.

I had the garden hose, on the bed of the truck, that was attached to the water tank! The hose was a fairly long garden hose as well, about a hundred yards in length. So I grabbed the end of the garden hose and raced up the hill, hose in hand, to cut off the fire before it reached the really large forest behind our house. Arriving at the spot where I wanted to start my fire barrier, to cut off the neck of the fire; I was starting to feel better about myself, in being so well-prepared to have such a long hose.

As I was trying to catch my breath from all the running I was doing, I looked down at the end of the garden hose to find no water coming out of the hose, like it needed to be. I even shook the hose vigorously, up and down, but nothing was coming out! Then it hit me, I had forgotten to turn the hose on, back at the tank! It's something I was learning out of this; small details do matter.

Sweat was now running down my face, as I ran back down to the truck; it was a lot of steps. Once back at the truck, I quickly turned the tap to the hose on, and made yet another back-to-back relay up the hill again. Confident that water would already be leaking out onto the ground when I got back up the hill as the tap was now turned on, I noticed that the fire kept creeping closer to my makeshift fire line, that was being formed in one of the rooms in my mind. There was no small amount of intensity. As I was making my way up the hill again, it was then, that I could see that I had some help coming my way. These reinforcements were my two older children, seven and eight years old. They had their water pistols in hand. *Good thing they are pretty good-sized water pistols,* I thought.

So as all three of us made it to the top of the hill, I instructed the kids where to start watering with their pistols: at the dry grass and the sticks in the woods. I grabbed the end of the garden hose, sweat pouring down my face and air struggling to enter my burning lungs of exhaustion, as I fought to catch my breath in-between wheezes. I stared at the end of the garden hose; but to my horror, not a single drop of water was coming out!

Bewildered, I quickly glanced over at the water tank sitting on the back of the truck. I could clearly see that the tank was full of water, and I knew the tap was now turned opened... perhaps the hose was plugged. So I shook the end of the hose some more.

If the hose is plugged, I'll need to find a screwdriver or something to wiggle in the end of it.

But this didn't seem to be a logical reason for the lack of water coming out of the hose, because I had been using the water tank and hose only twenty minutes earlier, to make sure it was in good working order. *This makes no sense... why is it not working even with my extra shaking of the hose?!*

At this point, my hands nervously combed through my hair once again, and another, *"AAHH!"* escaped from my lips, as I dropped to my knees and struggled to gain my composure and breath. I strained my brain to figure out what the problem was, as a level-three fear shot up to maximum capacity.

Then it occurred to me. It appeared that this water did not like running uphill, up through the hose. The end of the garden hose was higher than the top of the water tank, sitting on the back of the truck that was stuck in the mud at the bottom of the low, muddy area, a hundred yards away. This is why we need people like the McVanBucks in the world to bring knowledge to the nations. It is knowledge such as this that when you have a gravity-fed water hose, its end must be lower than the water tank unless you have a water pump... which I did not. Who needs a water pump when you have good plans in place?

As I ran back down the 100-yard line once again to the truck, Joy finally arrived on the scene. She had been gathering water buckets, for she could see my peril at hand. We unhooked the hose line and just started filling the buckets with water straight from the water tank, and then we hauled it up to the fire's edge.

Now, this was no small task to accomplish, for we had at least twenty yards of hard slugging through wet, soggy grass and mud. The weight of the water buckets dangling from our arms pulled us further down into the bog under our feet that was beneath the dead thistles. Each bucket felt like it weighed a ton.

This raised my fear level to level-four, with my feet now stuck in a bog, along with the water that was needed up the hill, a hundred yards away. Level-five fear was quickly closing in on me.

As the fire was about to enter the forest, my eight-year-old son came running up to me with level-five fear in his eyes, "Dad, what are we going to do?" he gasped.

I said, "Son, what I once learned from an neighbour, Mrs. Cooper, is that we pray."

And with that my son prayed and he said, "Dear God, help us!"

And with that, God did truly answer us almost immediately, for a neighbour came with water. He had a semi-truck tank full of several thousand gallons of water. He was a bit smarter too, for he drove his semi-truck through the neighbouring field on the high-side of the hill, to get to the fire. The neighbour was able to cut off the fire with his water hose and tank with ease, for his water-hose nozzle was three-inches wide and he had a water pump.

The fire died out, right on my imagined fire-line. With Joy and my children at my side, we thanked God that He gave us such good neighbours and answered my son's prayer.

A short while later, the familiar smell mixture of skunk and body odour filled my nose. The smell was creeping up behind me, like a ghost from the underworld, replacing the strong smell of smoke that hung in the air like a fog. There was no need to turn around to know that Mr. Brown had now also arrived to lend his helping hand.

Chapter Ten

⁂ *⁂*

Hole To The UnderWorld

I really do love living out in the country on our acreage. To me, this is a piece of paradise on earth -- when it's not up in flames. I did live in a city once; that lasted for only eight months.

Looking out my city window, about once a week, there he would be; my large, large neighbour, scruffy-faced, and all sprawled out on his couch in front of his living-room window, watching television with a drink in his hand. It must have been hot in his trailer home, for he was always only dressed in his cowboy hat and in his swimming trunks, but then again, they were more than likely just his underwear. It's not wise to look twice in moments like these, so I am only guessing here. In these types of situations, it's best to just shoot your eyes upwards and start whistling. This was not a pretty image for Joy, my wife, to shake out of her head at the best of times.

I had reminded Joy, "At least, the man has his underwear on, and don't forget... he's wearing a hat too."

She inquired, "Well, did you talk to him yet? He could at least close his blinds while he's cooling himself... like that!"

I had replied panting, "Well...I tried talking to him, but I didn't even reach the front door before his dog started chasing me. And he chased me for the next ten blocks."

Joy remarked, "Oh, I didn't know he got a new dog. What happened to the chihuahua?"

"No...no new dog, but I'll tell you, that little chihuahua is mean-spirited."

"Mentioning dogs, did you hear the other neighbour's dog last night? I really detest that annoying dog. He barked all night long, kept me awake," Joy said.

I replied, "Yeah, that outlaw dog, I believe, was right in our backyard again."

All that fine, city adventure with that dog and his crap on my lawn; no thanks. Which by springtime, I might add, the melting snow had revealed several large wet plops scattered about on my lawn. These plops could not have possibly been from a dog at all -- a plugged septic line, more likely, or a frightened Sasquatch, but you wouldn't suspect a dog, except that I had unfortunately seen the culprit with my own eyes.

Fresh country air is what I have now, as well as the gardening, and seeing our sheep grazing in the pasture, so I do not miss the city smog in the least.

There are hundreds of different things to do in the country, but there are some things that can be a little unpleasant, like the plugging up of a septic-tank pump.

One could pay someone else to fix it, but they have a way of charging you some insane price, for nine times out of ten, this plugging occurs on a holiday -- particularly Christmas day. And these unpleasant insane fees are just as bad as the plugged septic line itself, if not worse.

Now, if you don't mind getting your hands a little dirty, it would only cost you about forty bucks for the repair part at your local hardware store -- once they open four days after Christmas. Add a little self-taught experience and the ability to live in a sewer treatment plant for four days, and you have just saved yourself a bundle. Mind you, you would also have to survive the mob of family members that are ready to string you up, to save that bundle. Just remember to take the pressure out of the sewer line first, before popping that innocent-looking cover off, when your face is two inches from the covered line. Keeping your mouth closed and your tongue inside your mouth when that cover comes off, is also a very good idea. That stuff tastes just awful, but those are the draw-backs of saving a buck in the country.

By the time I was able to move out of the city and back to the countryside, I was, at least, a little bit prepared for the adventures that septic tanks can give a cheap person. I had witnessed how it was all supposed to be done by my good old dad Elvis; who, being a good, self-taught, cheap, country man, boldly led the way.

Dad would say, "Well...whadda we got here? Lemme open it and find out -- *Oops*." And then he would be hollering out, "Can't someone turn the water off!"

This one time in particular, I remember that my dad, Elvis, had a little problem with the septic tank. Looking back, the problem would have been a cheap investment if Dad had left it up to Plumber Dale to fix, who was a real professional. Instead, Dad tried fixing it on his own, and ended up in a tight spot.

It all began with the raw-sewer line backing up into our house. My basement bedroom was the first spot for the sewage to back-up into, and it got the heaviest load of the filth.

Just like all seventeen times before, within two minutes, I knew that we had a sewer problem, and I let the rest of my family know of the situation. Well, Dad went to work taking off covers, looking down lines, and peering into pumps to try to find out where the problem was.

Over the years, there had been other times that problems arose to cause grief to the country plumbing system. One such time was when Calvin flushed his teddy bear, Oscar, down the toilet in some sort of an attempt to give his teddy bear a wild, water-slide ride. This ride came to an abrupt end, when Oscar got plugged half-way down the sewer pipe. This act, of Calvin giving Oscar some much-needed entertainment -- in Calvin's eyes -- inadvertently created a damming effect as the liquids, solids, and used-toilet paper quickly built-up behind Oscar in the pipe.

This was repaired by Dad. First, he took a pipe apart, then he shoved his hand into the hole, and drug Calvin's teddy bear out to safety by it's head. This, at first, gave Calvin a great deal of excitement and happiness to see Oscar saved, but Calvin's delight quickly turned to a great deal of horror, disgust, and repulsion.

Calvin choked out, *"AHUUUHG*, Oscar's disgusting! What's that brown stuff stuck to him...?" And he scowled as his love quickly turned to hate, of his once-beloved Oscar.

The removal of Oscar from the pipe now allowed for the full-flow of the extras, which had been piling up behind Calvin's teddy, to flow with a free passage. Most of this sewage found its way down Dad's shirt, once it was relieved. It started flowing with a soft gurgle, then ended without warning with a big *"glub,"* in a sudden blast.

It was, at this point, that a flurry of unmentionable words came out of Dad's lips which I could see moving under the "wet dirt" that was dripping off of his face. One could not imagine that human manure has quite so many other repulsive and disturbing names attached to it, but apparently it does.

Now with this latest sewer back-up, after Dad did an extended search without finding a single problem, he came to the logical conclusion that the problem must be a plugged line. This plugged line was not visible from inside the house with one's naked-eye. The line that Dad was talking about led from inside the house to the

underground, septic holding tank, outside the house, next to the gravelled driveway. His attention was completely drawn to the inside of this septic tank, as being the source of this most recent nightmare of a problem that was unfolding inside the house basement.

Dad removed the large concrete cover-lid from the tank, and then began pumping the sewage out of the overflowing hole with a sub-pump. The
sub-pump siphoned the "grey water" up out of the sewer tank, through the hose, and spewed it into our sandbox, which we kids never played in that sandbox... ever again. *Better there than in my room,* I figured, *Who likes wet socks?... not me...*

Dad pumped out this raw sewage and it made its way out through the temporary, make-shift pump and hose; emptying the septic holding tank, so no more sewage would flow into my room.

After the tank was mostly pumped out with the spare sub-pump, Dad announced, "Well, the way I'm figurin' it, that line down there's plugged solid with another teddy bear."

At those words, my siblings and I gave Calvin a long, disgusted glare. *Man, it must be a really small teddy to plug up the two-inch line Dad's talking about,* I thought to myself. The two-inch opening to the end of the line was located near the bottom of the sewer-tank hole.

For several minutes, Mom and Dad stood in silence, peering down the disgusting, three-foot wide hole that went straight down, ten feet into the depths. This hole, which I perceived to be the hole to the underworld, was like a man-hole in a city street in many respects. The only difference was, this hole was situated behind our house, on our back lawn by the driveway.

Down in the sewer-tank hole, in the ten-foot deep space, the sewer tank split into two separate, holding tanks. The divider between the two tanks is a six-inch wide concrete wall, that kept the sewer "solids" on one side of the holding tank. On the other side of the wall is where the liquids, called "grey water," are temporarily held, before being pumped out into a nearby field or, as in this case, a sandbox. The name "grey water" is what nice people prefer calling the liquid, instead of calling it by its raw name, "liquid crap".

Now, if everything was working correctly at our house, the "grey water" from the one tank would get pumped through a small, two-inch hose out into the nearby field. And it was this little line that Dad was referring to, as being plugged by something.

Dad continued, "Somebody will have 'ta crawl down there 'n take a quick peek in that there line. Then get the heck outta there.

If'en it's plugged, I'll throw her down a screwdriver and then she can wiggle it in that there hole and it'll fix our problem. And one more thing... the whole time that person needs to be hold'n her breath, cause there's gotta be some pretty nasty gasses down there, that I suspect just might kill ya, if'en ya get a breath of it."

At this moment, Mom interrupted with a protest and a look of shock on her face... "If you think I'm crazy enough to go down there, you've got to be starving for madness and completely out of your mind."

Dad answered, "It's just a thought... just a thought. Maybe ya just might love me that much, to answer the call of duty."

Mom, in a disgusted tone, retorted, "I've put up with enough of your antics, and this crosses the line by a country mile. To think you'd put me in that filthy, stinky hole.... it's bound to end up being a grave."

After a moment of thought and silence, Dad said, "Well, I guess ya leave me no choice... one of ya kids like to go down there? I'll give ya a peppermint!" And he fished a green candy that was stuck to a couple of anti-acid tablets out of his pants pocket. "What, no takers?" with his hand extended. "Then I'll have to jemmy me-self down that there hole." Then he popped the whole lump of candy and anti-acids into his mouth.

"Very funny! I hope you're kidding me," Mom protested.

"No... I'm not kiddin' ... I'm not gonna to give up one of my dollars, to no plumber who fixes some dumb problem with his eyes closed. That just makes me look like some dumb idiot."

Mom knew that Dad could not be persuaded differently, once he got something stuck in his head.

Dad went on to explain his grand plan, "What we'll do here, is get that good ol' wooden ladder from the barn. Slip it down the hole, and stand it up there on that six-inch wall separatin' them two tanks. I'm thinkin' it should be wide 'nough to set the ladder on."

Mom cut into his wisely thought-out plan, to ask, "Elvis, you don't mean that wee, little ledge down there, do you? What if the ladder slips into the grey water, or worse, into the solid side? *Ekk*."

Dad was now irritated at Mom to suggest such a ridiculous thing, to think that the ledge was not wide enough for a ladder. Dad said, "Do ya mind? ....Ya didn't let me finish talk'n. I'll fasten the cow lasso 'round my waist. So that... if'en by slim chance... the ladder gets off that ledge, ya can simply pull me up. It'll also double fer a safety-rope. If'en something goes wrong with the ol' ladder, I can just climb up my lasso and back to safety."

Mom, knowing that Dad was now irritated and didn't like her trying to talk him out of something that would save them some money, didn't bother mentioning what she truly thought about the "good old wooden ladder," that had been left behind to rot in the yard by the previous owners of the farm. Mom hadn't considered the ladder to be a "bonus to their purchase," as Dad had tried pointed out at the time of buying the farm.

Dad had said, "See, this here… a free good ol' ladder… they've musta forgotten it? It's now ours! Whatta find!"

Mom's reply at the time was, "I believe that ladder was left here, to join this old cold house and that badly leaning barn. You sure the ladder's not holding up the barn from falling right on over?"

However, Mom now did attempt to point out that the ladder was way-past its prime, and the word "good" had been passed, by about eighty years. She thought that the rickety ladder could have easily been made by Methuselah himself, it was so old.

I suppose, Dad thought that the six rungs that looked to be "good," out of the total twenty rungs on the ladder, meant that this was a "good" twelve-foot ladder. It is a known fact, that according to most cheap farmers, any piece of equipment that is fifty percent “there” or greater, is considered to be “still good”.

Most of the rungs on this old ladder had a farmer’s fix-it-up; they had either baling twine or some sort of old tape, like maybe black electrical tape, wrapped around the broken rungs to hold them together. These were the rungs that remained, after not breaking all the way through, and they had sort of gotten a repair. The rest of the rungs were not there at all, and great gaps now showed in the ladder. Even a tall man would really have to stretch his legs over the large gaps, to get to the next repaired rung. Which, as Dad was not on the tall side, he really had to give a little extra stretch to reach the next rung.

The one good thing about the whole situation was that the cattle lasso rope, which Dad was intending to use, was the closest thing to being brand new, in the whole yard. The “good” old rope had been previously discarded, after having about fifty knots tied in it, to hold itself together.

At this point, Dad sent us kids in one direction to look for the old ladder and his new rope, while he went the other way to look around the barn.

After about an hour of tromping around, we kids remembered that we had borrowed the rope. We quickly returned it to our now-frustrated dad, who had been also looking for the rope and ladder, the entire hour.

"It was a good thing we had a good memory," we informed him, "and the rope wasn't working very well in our tree house, anyways."

We boys had abandoned using the rope, after we found out that it did not work well, in making a quick exit from the tree house. All it did was give us some terrible rope-burn to our hands when sliding down the rope in a hustle, like we had seen done in the movies.

The only thing that made us descend faster down the rope was when we needed to let go of the rope about halfway down, because the burning sensation from the rope-burn on the palms of our hands got too intense -- before all the flesh on our hands had burned off, altogether. The fall, from letting go of the rope, was not necessarily all that far.

It wasn't too painful for tough movie actors like ourselves, unless you were the first one down the rope. Then it was very painful, indeed, when your two younger brothers followed far too closely after you, like ninjas. And lacking the self-restraint to hang onto the rope that was burning their hands until they reached the halfway point before letting go, like I had done, they just simply let go. It was just a blur of boots and elbows. I think they might have just jumped straight out of the tree house, without even touching the rope, because those boots really hurt, when they came stomping down on my head.

We boys were quite impressed with the Hollywood actors. Those actors were sure tough to take that kind of pain to their hands and still be smiling for the movie camera. Maybe... we would need some more rope burns, built-up over time, then we could still be smiling at the end, like the actors did.

It was also at the tree house that we found the good old ladder, that we had borrowed from the barn.

Nedge exclaimed with excitement, “Hey, look! The ladder!”

I said, “Wow! Good eye, Nedge, good eye.”

We arrived back at the sewer hole a short time later with the ladder and rope like conquering heroes, but you could have sworn that Dad thought we had out-right “stolen” his ladder and rope. He did not need to yell quite that loudly at us, either... over just a simple, one or two month “borrow.” He did not even thank us for our good memory, when we boys were able to find his rope and ladder in less then two hours.

Once back at the sewer hole, all of the equipment was placed in their needed positions. Dad first needled a 2x6 board through the top rung of the ladder, and then he laid the board across the open mouth of the sewer hole. Wisely, this was done to help prevent the ladder from slipping too easily off the top of the little dividing ledge, ten feet down in the beast of filth. The ladder was now in the hole, and the cattle rope was tied around Dad's waist. Dad also had the needed screwdriver, in one hand, which he had retrieved from the nearby pickup truck. This screwdriver was essential to do the wiggling in the end of the line, to unplug the assumed plug-age at the bottom of the hole.

Dad instructed, as he threaded the rope through the top two rungs of the ladder, "...this here's how it's done, ya kids... pay attention, ya just might learn something."

I started to speak, "But, Dad, that tape on the ladder looks old-"

He abruptly cut my question off, "If I wanted your opinion, I would've asked ya... now listen up, this here's how it's done right," as he gave me a disgusted glare.

Dad then turned his attention back to Mom and began explaining his plan, "Now, ya hold onto this end of the rope, and keep her tight while I make my way down. Just remember, if there's any trouble, ya'll have to pull me outta there in a hurry... or I'll be pushin' up daisies with my ten toes, if those gases get me, ha... ha."

Then he took a gigantic breath, his cheeks

puffing out much like a squirrel with a handful of seeds stuffed in its cheeks, and Dad began to descend into the hole. Carefully, he slipped past the safety board that was laying across the mouth of the hole, and he began to make his way down the rickety ladder. Struggling to stretch his legs over the large gaps in the ladder, he reached the bottom of the ladder; and stood, balancing on the slippery little six-inch concrete, dividing wall.

Huddling around the top of the sewer-tank hole, Mom and us kids leaned forward, intent on keeping our eyes on Dad. We could see that he was trying to bend over, in an effort to get his head low enough to see inside the suspected problem line that was near his feet. He was wanting to see if he needed to give his screwdriver a wiggle in the end of the line, to clean it out if it was plugged. But he couldn't get a good look at the end of the line, for the width of the sewer hole didn't give him the needed space for him to bend his head down, low enough to see inside, without hitting his head against the slimy side-walls of the hole. As we watched, we could see Dad's head slowly become a deep-red colour from the lack of air.

Concerned, Daisy spoke up, "Mom?"

"U-m-m, yes, Daisy?"

"How long can Dad hold his breath down

there?"

Mom replied, sort of worriedly, "I don't know, but the way his red face is looking down there, I don't think he's got much longer!"

A moment later, we could see that Dad had now abandoned trying to wrench his head over to see into the problem line. He had even abandoned the screwdriver-wiggling idea. With his face bright-red and his eyes bulging, he was now trying to escape the hole from the underworld. He was desperately trying to make an all-out effort to get to some much-needed air, above ground.

Scrambling to make his way up the old ladder, in his haste, Dad did not quite step over the large gap in the ladder. This was due to his mind being blurred because of the lack of oxygen and him clunking his head against the insides of the walls, two or three times. In his panicked, muddled state-of-mind, his foot completely missed the really large gap that was about three-fourths of the way up the ladder.

Dad's deep-red head only briefly emerged above the top of the hole as he sucked in a single gasp of fresh air. Then his foot missed the next rung, and gravity stripped the ladder's gears, as Dad was kicked into reverse.

As he unexpectedly began his rapid

descent, his chin clipped each rickety rung that was left on the old ladder. Breaking through all the remaining rungs of the ladder, except for the really solid ones, Dad's chin made a *clack-clack-clack...WHACK-clack* sound as he soared down to the bottom of the ladder. This enlarged the gaping hole in the ladder, making it impossible for him to climb back up. The ladder now looked more like a pair of rickety stilts.

Thankfully, when Dad fell back down the ladder, his crotch landed on the six-inch wide, concrete wall.

This abruptly stopped his body from continuing down into the very bottom of the sewer tank liquids, that would have been well over his head, even if he landed feet-first. Dad landed with one of his legs dangling on either side of the concrete wall.

As he hit this obstruction with his crotch, Dad was forced to cry out with a loud uncontrollable howl, "P-O-O-*O-W-H-Owwaaoohohoho,*" as his full set of false teeth shot out of his mouth like a cannon ball from the force of wind that was still hanging around in his lungs.

This surprise force of wind that came out of his lungs, caused him to then suck in a large breath of bad air at the bottom of the hole, well-below his desired destination, above ground. He sucked in the toxic fumes inside the hole, while, at the same time, pony-riding a concrete wall without a soft saddle. Stunned and dazed, Dad now just sat, perched uncomfortably on the six-inch wall.

Then we heard a muffled roar from inside the hole, coming from the lips of a toothless man, "Get me outta here! I think I'm gonna faint from all these poison fumes!"

When Dad had descended back down the ladder unexpectedly, the safety rope we all had been holding, sizzled hot through our hands, forcing us to let go of his safety rope. Now in panic, we five kids and Mom all grabbed up the rope again. We pulled for all we were worth, but we could not pull Dad up, even with all the added adrenaline pumping through us like jolts of lighting. People can be really heavy when trying to pull them up, out of a hole.

Good thing Mom was a crazy-fast thinker, as she had a steady stream of antics that gave her the needed experience to save the day and her Elvis's life. I guess, this well-trained gift had come by experience with all the horrific fires she had witnessed first-hand, not because Mom was a firefighter by trade, but by a forced-draft caused in a large part by her dear Elvis and us rascals for kids.

Realizing by now, that there was no way we were going to be able to pull up a dazed, fainting man on his last breath, Mom grabbed the end of the rope from our hands, and ran like the wind to the nearby green 4x4 pick-up truck. She wrapped the rope around the steel, pickup truck bumper, and then she jumped into the truck. Even though this was an ingenious idea, there were some small problems with her hasty, fast-thinking plan.

For starters, one of these small problems was that Mom wasn't aware that the other end of the cattle rope, which had originally been tied around Dad's waist, now had slid down to his ankles. This had occurred as the rope slackened, when we had all temporarily let go of it for a moment, as it burned through our hands, when Dad had missed the rung with his foot and made his unwanted descent to the bottom of the ladder. He was able to at least get back onto his feet, by standing on the little separating wall. The rope then became snug around the groggy man's ankles, as the truck moved forward; then a second little problem was revealed.

Dad's safety board, laying over the mouth of the sewer hole, was still under one of the remaining rungs of the ladder. As Mom quickly popped the clutch, the truck lurched forward, spitting bits of gravel over our heads. The gravel rained down into the hole, on Dad's head... we kids should've told him that the gravel was coming his way.

But with such little time to speak, we could

only watch in helpless dismay. Dad had been watching as well, looking upwards for help out of the hole, when the gravel came raining down into his eyes. Dad blurted out, "ME' EYES!" As the truck lurched forward, it instantly removed the slack from the rope, and then began pulling Dad up fast. It was then that Dad's safety board slipped from the top of the hole, and started falling down into the hole.

It was about at this point, that a full-dose of adrenaline kicked into my body, as everything around me went into slow motion.

I heard a groggy voice, with real fear in it, coming out of the hole, "BUT WAIT, The Rope is... is, B-w-a-a-a...t!"

But these muffled words, Mom failed to hear over the truck's running engine and the flying gravel. As the rope pulled Dad up out of the hole, feet first, one more of Dad's great safety features was revealed; he had looped the rope around though the top rung of the ladder, also.

As he came soaring up and out of the hole, he was uttering words from his toothless gums that sounded like, *"Mumma-mee-W-w-a-a-u-h-h-w! Ouch!"*

He came out of the sewer hole, feet first. To me, Dad looked just like a giant fish being pulled out of an ice-fishing hole, by it's tail. The safety board that had fallen down into the hole, had met Dad when he was about halfway up and slipped under the back of Dad's shirt, until its nose peeked out of the neck hole.

The other end of the safety board then got wedged-fast in the top rung of the ladder, as it was now rising up out of the hole in unison with Elvis's rising body. Only the top two rungs of the ladder, which had avoided being broken by Dad's chin, remained in place.

Guided by the rope around his ankles, Dad's feet slipped into the space between the two top rungs of the ladder, where he had originally threaded the rope. This gap was too tiny for a body of Elvis's size; nevertheless, his chubby little body was being squeezed through this top hole in the ladder. With the safety board still attached to his back, he kind of looked like a lump of bread being poked into an oven. Unfortunately, Dad's body was not going to squeeze all the way through, between the two rungs, and the ladder got stuck around his chest area. His arms were stretched up beside his head, like they were pinned to his ears. He now looked like a big hog on a campfire spit, speared through and ready for roasting.

Then the whole contraption burst out of the hole: the rope, ladder, safety board, and Dad, and crashed down onto the safe ground beside the hole. The broken ladder made, what appeared to be (to the eyes of a little kid) a giant pair of scissors, snipping on a loaf of bread. The ladder also gave the illusion of an angry alligator's jaws, chomping down on the man named Elvis. This chomping could have been avoided, had Mom stopped the truck much sooner, and would have saved him at least three or four chomps from the broken ladder. But in an emergency, when death is so close at hand, who could think about such details?

Mom finally stopped the truck, when she saw that her husband was now freed from the mouth of the hole. Jumping out of the truck, she rushed over with the rest of us kids, to see if Dad was still alive or not.

Her voice quivering, she managed to croaked out, "Elvis... speak to me! Are you dead?" We all stared down at the muddy-faced toothless man laying before us.

Dad, moaning and groaning painfully, replied with a distinctive toothless slur, "No... no... I live, I think, or ya'll are the saddest lookin' angels I ever saw. Untangle me from this mess now, would ya?"

With all of us helping, we soon figured out how to untangle him from all the broken pieces of wooden ladder, board, and rope.

Dad was very stinky and filthy, the only clean spots on his face that we could see were the whites of his eyes and his pink flapping tongue and gums. Mom insisted on spraying him down with the garden hose, to rinse off a couple of thick layers of slimy "grey water" that was sticking to his body, before he took a bath.

Once Dad was somewhat rinsed off by the garden hose, he sat on the ground while Mom cleaned up his wounded chin and belly which had taken quite a painful beating. She cleaned them up with some peroxide that Daisy had retrieved from the house for her. The quick exit from the sewer hole had opened up Dad's tender underbelly when the buttons on his shirt got torn off, when he was dragged up the side of the tank wall. (I heard that the hair on Dad's chest eventually did grow back – in patches. At least, there had been that slimy sludge on the sides of the tank hole, to lessen the friction of the melting buttons.)

As Dad sat there, with his shredded shirt wide-open and a stunned look on his dripping-wet face, Mom finally spoke, "After all of these antics of yours, Elvis... for a stupid sewer line that's still plugged. I am going to call Plumber Dale at the Sewer Master Company."

Dad replied, "No...No, ya won't have to do that...I think I'm a'seeing what the problem is."

"You must be a mad man, if you're thinking of going back down there again, to save a buck!" Mom protested with shock written all over her face at the sheer cheapness of her man.

Still catching his breath, he spoke, "No... not that. Sittin' here, I can see the electric plug-in fer the sewer pump over there, that goes to the house and it's... it...well... it's unplugged! I must'a unplugged the electricity to the sewer pump yesterday, when I plugged the grain drying fan in. Maybe someone should plug the pump back in. This, I'm thinkin'... will fix the misdiagnosed, plugged sewer line in this here hole of death... and for cryin' out loud, I'm blowin' our life savings and buyin' a new ladder, a shirt, and some new teeth from town today! 'Less one of ya kids wannna jimmy-down there, in that there's hole and find my teeth. I'll even give ya a peppermint," as he pulled out a handful of slime-covered peppermints from his pocket.

About the Author

*

You can find more information about Peter N. Mast and his future writings on his website, www.mcvanbuck.com. He hopes to release the sequel to McVanBuck Call Of The Lighter in 2021, with a few more stories and a few more laughs.

Manufactured by Amazon.ca
Bolton, ON

14306292R00129